**Look what people are saying about Meg Maguire's
latest title, Making Him Sweat!**

"Maguire succeed... ...a sterling combo
of love... ...d tears.

—... ...ws

"M... ...irst book in a brand new
series... ...that centres around MMA.
You k... ...at means, right? Hot, sweaty,
half n... men. I'm there. I can expect only
good things from Maguire!"
—*Under the Covers*

"If you enjoy reading about super sexy boxers
who like to get down and dirty, then
definitely give this book a try."
—*Blithely Bookish*

"[F]ull of interesting, likable characters
and sexy love scenes."
—*Fiction Vixen*

"I loved this book! Jenna and Mercer share
some delicious sexual tension, but thankfully
Ms Maguire does not torture her readers.
I definitely recommend this book and am
looking forward to reading the sequel."
—*Badass Book Reviews*

"I love fight books...especially where old school
boxing meets the more modern MMA style.
This cute book had so many great characters and a

TAKING HIM DOWN

BY
MEG MAGUIRE

First published in Great Britain 2013
by Mills & Boon, an imprint of Harlequin (UK) Limited,
Eton House, 18-24 Paradise Road, Richmond, Surrey TW9 1SR

© Meg Maguire 2013

ISBN: 978 0 263 90515 1

30-0813

Harlequin (UK) policy is to use papers that are natural, renewable and recyclable products and made from wood grown in sustainable forests. The logging and manufacturing processes conform to the legal environmental regulations of the country of origin.

Printed and bound in Spain
by Blackprint CPI, Barcelona

Before becoming a writer, **Meg Maguire** worked as a record-store snob, a lousy barista, a decent designer and an overenthusiastic penguin handler. Now she loves writing sexy, character-driven stories about strong-willed men and women who keep each other on their toes… and bring one another to their knees. Meg lives north of Boston with her husband. When she's not trapped in her own head, she can be found in the kitchen, the coffee shop or jogging around the nearest duck-filled pond.

For Ruthie and Serena, cherished sparring partners
in all things wonked and wordy.

And thanks, as always, to my editor, Brenda.
Don't mess with her—she's been trained.

1

"NOT TIGHT ENOUGH. Start over."

Though the guy suppressed his frustration well, Rich knew he was getting cussed out in the privacy of the teenager's head.

Tough shit, kid. Get yourself a paid fight and you can be the colossal dick for a night.

The gauze was obediently unwound from Rich's palm, the elaborate process started all over.

Mercer cut through the locker room chaos carrying a tub of Vaseline. According to the promotional materials, he was Rich's trainer. In truth, Rich trained himself. He liked it that way, not having to answer to anybody. But after tonight he'd be committing to a manager, landing a deal with a major mixed martial arts organization. He'd get hauled out of Boston and obscurity and shipped out west to train under a team of MMA specialists. Saddled with a half dozen guys riding his back about every mile he ran, every forkful of food or drop of booze that passed his lips, every last detail that led up to him stepping into the ring.

Oh frigging well. Price of success.

"You look good," Mercer said, crouching and unscrewing the tub's lid.

"You look real pretty, too, Merce."

"You look *calm*. If you're faking it, keep it up." He smeared Rich's temples, cheeks and forehead, to reduce the friction when he took a shot to the face.

When Rich's hands were finally wrapped and taped to his satisfaction, Mercer passed him his fingerless MMA gloves.

"Where's your mouth guard?"

"Quit fussing, grandma—I got everything organized. Go celebrate for a few minutes." Mercer's actual trainee, Delante, had won his first real pro fight twenty minutes earlier, with a skull-thumper of a closing punch. "Get that kid cleaned up for the press and tell him not to mumble."

"Fine. I'll be back." Mercer slapped Rich's shoulder and took off.

Rich tugged on his gloves, gave his fists a squeeze. Nice and snug. He liked the feeling with the medical tape in place, that promise of a proper scrap, no sparring tonight.

He was a good fighter—a hell of a good fighter, if you factored in how DIY his regimen was—but he had more than that going. He was six-three and had made weight at 204. He was built and goddamn good-looking, and had what his late mentor called "the magic." That thing you can't build in a gym or find in a supplement bottle. That thing that made guys want to hit you and made their girlfriends want to wake up in your bed.

Nobody respected a pretty face inside the ring, and that suited Rich fine. Whatever had people hungry to see him lose, bring it on. Whatever had opponents hating him for winning, whatever had promoters eager to give him another match. Love and hate felt the same when you were high on adrenaline, and your detractors shelled out the same money for tickets as your fans did. That hate-ability plus a solid win tonight and Rich would get signed. Give it nine months and a couple decent matches and he'd be on the magazine covers, courted by equipment and vitamin companies for the right to slap his face on their ads. Whether it'd still be so pretty by then…

Didn't matter. Rich would win, he'd sign, his future manager would handle the offers. He'd suck it up and take whatever orders his training team barked, and he'd be successful. Of that, he had no doubt.

But he wasn't hungry for that—fame or attention.

He was hungry for a fight, sure. That was a perk. But the thing that lit a fire in his gut, made him salivate for this moment, was the money.

Fifteen grand when he won tonight. Down the road, once he signed—twenty, thirty, fifty and up, plus the endorsement deals. And he'd lease his face to whoever offered him the fattest checks, and cash them with no qualms.

It might not be honorable, but Rich Estrada fought for money. Because fighting was the thing he was good at, the diploma he'd never earned, the only marketable talent he had.

He fought because if he didn't, his mom would be dead inside a year.

THE ARENA WAS in turns dim and blinding, the air pungent with a hundred clashing aromas. Lindsey Tuttle was planted in the thick of it, three rows from the action and close enough to hear every kick and punch and grunt.

The cage was eight-sided, walled in by chain-link, and it held two bloodthirsty opponents—just names off a fight card, men Lindsey didn't know beyond their records and vital stats.

She leaned in toward her boss and friend, Jenna, to shout-whisper, "Who's winning?"

"I dunno." On closer inspection, she saw that Jenna's eyes were squeezed shut. It seemed she'd reached her capacity for spectating during the previous match, watching with her hands clamped to her mouth as her boyfriend, Mercer's young protégé, had won his first big fight. It hadn't been too bloody—a lot of rolling around, then one wince-worthy punch that sprayed red across Delante's opponent's cheek. It had dropped the guy's limbs like deadweight and had the ref announcing a knockout halfway through the third round.

Lindsey watched the two strangers grappling under the lights. There was no commentary to explain what was happening, and she wasn't sure which of the guys tangled on the ground was pinned, and which was doing the pinning.

But damn, it was exciting.

It was the fourth fight of the night, the big-deal bouts still to come. Lindsey worked for Jenna's matchmaking company in Chinatown, and their office was located one floor above the mixed martial arts gym Mercer managed. Aside from Delante, the only fighter Lindsey knew from the gym was slated for the third-to-last match. She glanced at his name on the fight card. *Rich Estrada.*

She shivered.

But only because she didn't want her acquaintance getting his face broken. Not because Rich's huge, alarming body gave her…*feelings.* Most certainly not. He was singularly the most obnoxious man she'd met in ages.

As shouts rose all around her, she realized she'd spaced out. The crowd roared, but with delight or disappointment? Men's emotions all wound up sounding the same if you doused them with enough testosterone and alcohol.

A winner was proclaimed, his sweaty arm hoisted by the ref.

If Rich won his match, he stood a chance of "escaping the dungeon," as Mercer had worded it—moving on to bigger and better things than toiling all day in the subterranean sweatbox also known as Wilinski's Fight Academy. It had been a respected boxing gym in the eighties when Jenna's dad, Monty, had opened it, but after a criminal scandal and the sport's decline in popularity, the place had gone to seed.

Now Mercer was at the helm, saddled with the unenviable task of bringing it back into legitimacy with the addition of MMA training and some overdue improvements. Delante and Rich winning their matches could do wonders, he'd said. Bragging rights were everything in this business.

"I need a drink," Jenna said, eyes finally open. Her face was pale. This was clearly not her sport. Too bad she'd fallen in love with Mercer. His years as an amateur boxer had left him with a misshapen nose and cauliflower ears, and Jenna must have been imagining it was his face being pounded every time a strike landed.

She rose and Lindsey rooted in her wallet for a ten. "Get me a beer?"

"Sure."

Lindsey was enjoying the exotic atmosphere. Cleaners had to disinfect the ring between matches, mopping away the blood and sweat, and the air was charged with adrenaline. She'd grown up in a family of hockey fanatics, but with hockey, the fights were a bonus—icing on a cupcake. MMA was nothing but frosting.

As the prefight prep wound down, her fascination shifted. Rich's match followed the next one. Her energy dropped low, humming in her belly.

Just nervous for him, she told herself, nearly believing it.

Rich was a handsome, fearless showman, the center of his own universe. And he was annoying enough simply *acting* as though Lindsey must be in awe of him when he swung by their office to flirt. He'd surely be insufferable if he found out she had an actual crush on him, as superficial and physical as it was.

Superficial and physical and *inconvenient.* She was supposed to be trying to make her current relationship work.

Work being the operative word. Relationships shouldn't *be* work at twenty-seven. They should be fun and natural.

But things with Brett were exhausting and serious, and if she wasn't mistaken, they were moving backward. They'd gotten engaged before relocating from Springfield to Boston. He'd moved to take his first law job and she'd followed after securing her own gig as a wedding planner. He'd broken the engagement after one month of cohabitation. Nothing like faking adoration for other women's diamond rings right after packing your own away in the back of your sock drawer.

They'd needed to slow things down. Too many changes, too soon, he'd said. New city, new career, new home…*old girlfriend,* she'd inferred. A girlfriend who'd sufficed when Brett had been a broke student, but didn't seem to be cutting it now. She knew that whatever he felt about the old apartments he'd lived in and his former identity as a kind, lovable dork…he now felt the same about her, too. They'd been friends since eighth grade, confidants through high school and finally a couple when Brett came back to Western Mass for law school. That history had been the backbone of their romance. But Lindsey had borne witness to the old Brett, and it seemed the new, polished, hotshot Brett resented her for it. It made living with him a daily struggle.

Jenna returned, handing Lindsey a plastic pint of beer and a wad of change.

"Thanks."

Jenna sat and gulped half her red wine in one swallow.

Lindsey laughed. "You're going to make the worst fight wife ever."

"Don't tell me you're actually enjoying this?"

"Oh, God, yeah. I have no idea how to tell who's winning, once they get rolling around on the ground, but it's still fun. Plus…you know. Half-naked sweaty men."

Jenna shot her a squirrelly look. During a wine-soaked working lunch the previous week, Jenna had weaseled the Brett situation out of Lindsey. She normally liked to keep her

personal life personal, but that was hard when your boss—
and best friend in a new city—was pathologically romantic.

Last week, Lindsey and Brett had been on-again. As of
three nights ago they were off-again, to the tune of a mutually negotiated free-to-see-other-people experiment. They
still cared for each other, but as friends now, more than lovers. She'd poured years of love and energy into what they had,
but it had begun to feel like an obligation, not a commitment.

"Brett doesn't care if I look at other guys," she assured
Jenna. Let her think they were still together if it made her
happy. "You're not one of those types who think checking
people out is cheating, I hope?"

"I'm not *that* old-fashioned."

"It's a very pervy sport," Lindsey said with approval. "Our
payback for women's beach volleyball uniforms."

"You perv all you want, but I'm keeping my eyes shut.
They ought to make special blurry glasses, so you can't see
the blood."

After a noisy introduction, the next match began.

The guys seemed to be getting bigger, the crowd more
excited. Lindsey felt the energy herself, an electric stirring
in her middle, not quite fear, not quite arousal, but as primal as both.

No shoes, no shirts, fingerless gloves. Muscular men rolling around. She scanned the crowd, surprised by how few
women were in the audience. Then the guy on the mat took an
elbow to the face and the resulting blood reminded her why
that was. Jenna hissed with fear, squinting through her bangs.

But Lindsey leaned forward, mesmerized.

The very concept was thrilling—two humans stripped
and tossed in a ring, out to prove which one was the stronger, better competitor with a minimum of rules, etiquette
and padding. Lots of blood and sweat, surely lots of bruises
when dawn arrived. Lots of…skin. Lots of everything she

was missing out on since Brett had ripped his new, urbane identity out of an *Esquire* spread.

The match ended with an anticlimax, the outcome decided by the judges. Next up, the third-to-last fight, yet as far as Lindsey was concerned, the main event.

She watched the ring prep, heart thumping harder, harder, until she swore she could hear it over the rabble. She twisted her program into a tight tube again and again.

"Rich is next," Jenna said, the collar of her shirt fisted in both hands. "Why couldn't Mercer be into fly-fishing? Or ultimate Frisbee?"

"Too bad you didn't inherit your dad's love of fighting, huh?"

Instead, Jenna had inherited the gym, along with a portion of the former factory that housed it. She'd been estranged from her dad but had moved to Boston to take advantage of her odd inheritance sight-unseen and open a new franchise of Spark, a regional matchmaking company. Lindsey was awfully happy she had. She liked her new job. In fact, she'd probably *love* it, once her own romantic hangover subsided. At the moment it wasn't the easiest thing, mustering enthusiasm for other people's relationships.

"I just don't get it," Jenna said, blue eyes on the activity in the ring.

Lindsey shrugged. "Mercer will never get matchmaking. It's healthy to have some autonomy." Did she believe that for real? Or was she just trying to make herself feel better about how much space she craved from Brett?

The announcer scattered her thoughts.

"Next up, the match to decide the New England MMA Light Heavyweight Championship!" Music started up and the gigantic arena screen displayed two open double doors.

"In the blue corner, defending his title, a mixed martial artist from Warwick, Rhode Island. Thirty-one years old, five feet eleven inches, two hundred and five pounds. Greg 'the Trucker' Higgins!"

Striding down the aisle toward the cage, Higgins was meaty and pink-faced, with a tacky chinstrap beard and a trucker cap that helped explain his fight name. Several men in matching hats and shirts followed.

Jenna clapped politely. Lindsey hated Higgins out of principle, and booed along with the minority as he strutted to Johnny Cash's "I've Been Everywhere, Man." He stripped to his shorts and entered the ring, warming up as his music faded.

"A-a-a-nd in the black corner, a boxer and kickboxer hailing from Lynn, Massachusetts. Twenty-eight years of age, six feet three inches, two hundred and four pounds, Rich 'Prince Richard' Estrada!"

Her breath hitched when Rich appeared on-screen. She twisted in her seat to watch him descend. His intro music was a remixed hybrid of hoity-toity chamber music and some infectious Latin hip-hop. He wore black warm-up pants and an open, deep purple sweatshirt lined with ermine fleece, hood cocked. Raising his arms, he welcomed the modest applause, and hisses from the Higgins fans. He dropped his hood with a grand, arrogant gesture and bared his chest, fists thrust triumphantly in the air, his entire body emanating 10,000 watts of pure, blinding smugness.

Mercer trailed him, along with a couple other guys Lindsey recognized from Wilinski's, his corner for the fight. Unlike Higgins, Rich's team didn't have special gear splashed with sponsor logos, just black T-shirts with Wilinski's Fight Academy, Boston, silk-screened on the front.

"This match will be comprised of three five-minute rounds," the announcer confirmed for the fans.

Rich stripped and Mercer shoved a mouth guard between his lips. When one of the guys from Wilinski's slicked his arms and chest with Vaseline, Lindsey suppressed a ridiculous stab of jealousy. He entered the ring to warm up and the lights over the audience went dark as the music faded, setting Lindsey's skin prickling.

The men fought barefoot. Higgins wore loose-fitting kick-boxing trunks covered in sponsorship logos. Rich sported far snugger, plainer shorts, ones that hugged his thighs and butt and…other places, and made Lindsey feel funny. Dangerous-funny.

The men hopped and shadowboxed, keeping their muscles primed as the rules were announced. When Rich circled she could see the large tattoo inked between his shoulder blades in black and gray. The dark wingspan of a condor above a shield, framed by draped banners—the Colombian national crest, a snoop through the MMA message boards had told her. He had a mismatched design on the swell of his right shoulder—a circular field showing a river and horizon, an ax, an anchor—the seal of his hometown. There was a third one, a line of black Thai characters that ran down his ribs. Lindsey didn't know what they said, only that he'd trained in Thailand for a year. All indelible reminders of where he'd come from, or perhaps souvenirs of where he'd been. Apt for a man destined to go places.

What must it feel like, being in the spotlight, everyone's eyes on you? Lindsey had always been a supporting player, tagging behind her popular older sisters when she was growing up; a barnacle along for the voyage when she'd uprooted her life to follow Brett. For her past clients, the invisible woman running herself ragged so their big days would go off without a hitch, and for her future clients, the temporary go-between broker, there to facilitate their first dates.

As she watched Rich stretching his neck and shoulders, bathed in those pure white beams…she envied him. She'd never felt like someone whose entrance commanded the room's attention, let alone an entire arena. Lindsey was always in the shadows, never the light, frequently thanked but never applauded.

A blonde ring girl in a spangly bra-top circled the cage, flashing a sign that read Round 1. There was no bell. Instead the official shouted, "Let's go!" and the men met in the center for a second's grudging fist tap before jumping back, circling.

Neither was shy. Both kept their guards up, feet busy. Rich baited his opponent with a couple short jabs, rewarded when Higgins took a swing. Rich dodged it and came back with a kick to Higgins's thigh, then crowded him toward the chain-link.

They traded minor hits, then Higgins escaped and retreated a few paces. Rich stayed on him, still baiting, getting him to toss out defensive jabs, sneaking in a punch here, a kick there when his opponent's guard was open. For a while, the action seemed to slow. Higgins certainly seemed to slow, shifting from foot to foot, red in the face.

Just when the fight was starting to get a bit boring—*bam*. Rich caught Higgins with a high kick to his ear. It bent the guy over, and Rich got him in the back of the knee and buckled him. Then, chaos.

Rich was on his opponent, pummeling his head and raised arms with punches and elbow strikes, hard enough that Lindsey saw sweat or spittle flying under the lights. The crowd was roaring. She realized she was screaming herself, a stream of hysteria erupting from some well of untapped ferocity.

Mercer stalked the periphery of the cage, shouting and jabbing the air. Lindsey wondered if Jenna was going to get soundly trounced tonight, and if so, she envied her. She could use a sound trouncing herself. Hell, she'd take a spirited dry-humping.

Higgins managed to get his legs around Rich's waist and

shift them to their sides, but the effort looked desperate. Rich took a sharp hook to the temple, unfazed.

An air horn blasted to end the round, and Rich was on his feet. Higgins wasn't quite so quick to rise, and Rich wasn't as courteous as some of the earlier fighters—he didn't offer his opponent a hand up. Both made it back to their corners. Through the fence, Lindsey watched Mercer swab Rich's now bleeding temple with some kind of goo, another guy forcing a water bottle to his lips.

Her heart thudded so hard she felt high. She wished she were right there, close enough to smell him and see whatever fearsome energy was shining in his dark eyes.

The ring girl did her prancy thing, then the round began. The men swapped punches and kicks. Lindsey hadn't even taken two breaths and *whack!* A stunningly hard hook from Rich and Higgins went to all fours. Rich followed, ready to grapple, but an official stepped in and forced him away. There seemed to be a short window of time during which everyone waited for Higgins to make it to his feet, but it didn't happen. He dropped his forehead to the mat between his elbows, body shifting uneasily from side to side, and suddenly—

"A stoppage has been called, due to a technical knockout." The crowd erupted in a mix of cheers and boos. Rich was corralled to the center by the ref, and once his opponent was helped to standing—

"The winner—Rich Es-s-strada!"

His arm was raised, and Lindsey shrieked like a banshee. Jenna caught up, looking confused but thrilled, having missed the single punch that had ended the round inside fifteen seconds. The earlier shot Rich had taken must have been worse than it had looked. A thin ribbon of red trailed from his temple down to his jaw. The announcer held the mike between them and asked, "How does it feel, earning your first championship title?"

Between panting breaths, Rich answered, "Overdue."

"Good fight?"

"If I ever get another match with Higgins, I want a scrap next time, not a slow dance."

This was met with major heckling from the Trucker fans.

"Any other words?"

He put his hands on his hips, chest still heaving. "Thank you, Merce, all you guys. Thank you, *Mamá*. Thank you, Diana. And thank you, Monty, wherever you wound up." He gave a little heavenward salute and walked away from the mike.

As Rich stepped down from the raised ring, Mercer greeted him with a beaming smile that seemed to ask, "What took you so long?" They shared a manly, brusque hug before a medical guy tidied Rich's cut. Rich led the way back up the aisle, his corner following. Lindsey's gaze caught on his back muscles, gleaming under the stark spotlight.

"Wow," she said, relaxing back in her seat.

"If only all fights were that efficient." Jenna frowned. "Except that would mean every fight ended with someone getting really badly hurt."

"Still. What a way to kick off your career." In a few months, Lindsey could be shelling out a small fortune to watch Rich fight on pay-per-view. The thought was enlivening, except…

Something soured her stomach. Rich wouldn't be around much longer. Mercer had said he needed new guys to fight, more opponents in his weight class and at his level. He'd be off to a training camp, who knew where.

She'd miss Rich's ego-stroking flirtation, but it had been nice while it lasted. Exciting, without any messy romantic fallout. A crush. Someone to get secretly nervous about seeing, to put on eyeshadow for, without actually having to do any of the work of an actual relationship. Then again, also without getting to enjoy any of the perks, such as three rounds with Rich's body in the ring better known as her bed.

As if she'd have had the first clue what to do with him if she got the chance.

With Delante's and Rich's victories secured, the final two matches were stress-free. By the time the main event was wrapped, Lindsey had officially caught the MMA bug. Swearwords she'd never uttered aloud had come streaming from her mouth unbidden, and she'd hopped to her feet so many times it was a wonder she hadn't broken a heel or twisted her ankle.

"Are you coming to the after party?" Jenna asked, organizing her purse. "Nothing glamorous, but free drinks once the press stuff is done. Merce and I could give you a lift later."

"Count me in. I could stand a little VIP treatment." It wasn't every day she'd get a chance to mingle in this strange, feral world.

If she'd known she'd be going to an after party, she'd have dressed up a bit more. It was chilly for early fall and she'd worn jeans. Nice ones, with a cute top, but watching jacked, angry men attack each other had her feeling exceptionally feminine, and she wished she'd dressed to reflect that.

Jenna had a pass to get them behind the scenes, and they followed the noise and activity to the threshold of a boardroom past the lockers. A long table was set up at the far end of the room with microphones, and the fighters sat behind it, all showered and dressed, answering questions for the small cluster of press people. Rich had changed into a suit, and Lindsey could make out the white bandage someone had applied to his temple.

Most of the questions were for the bigger-name guys from the final matches. But when one reporter asked Rich how he felt about his "lucky punch," he smirked and replied, "If this was archery, you wouldn't be asking about my lucky bull's-eye."

When the meeting disbanded, Lindsey and Jenna followed the crowd. They ended up in a fancy area for the corporate types who had box seats and season tickets, and the open bar was swamped. They spotted Mercer loading stuff onto a dolly, presumably to be taken back to Wilinski's. Jenna hugged her boyfriend, and Mercer's return embrace looked eager and possessive, making Lindsey a touch envious. She hadn't felt the pleasant dig of strong male fingers at her back in ages.

The couple broke apart, and Lindsey clapped Mercer's arm in congratulations. "Happy, I trust?"

He laughed. "There's an understatement."

"What do you think—was it a lucky punch?"

"Rich doesn't need luck. He hits like a truck."

"Do you wish he'd gotten a chance to show what else he can do?"

Mercer shook his head. "Nah. Rich has that thing—that thing people love to hate. He'll be even more of a draw if fans are dying for his win to be proven a fluke."

"Where is he?"

"Being courted by managers, same as Delante. I need to get over there myself, keep an eye on the kid. You girls should get some drinks—I'm driving."

Lindsey and Jenna hit the bar, then wound up loitering in the concourse with a small group of guys who trained at Wilinski's. They spent some time getting to know their mysterious, violent neighbors and trying to follow the post-fight gossip.

A bit later Jenna disappeared in search of Mercer, and Lindsey was starting to feel the hour, her adrenaline waning. She took a seat on a radiator, letting her heels drop to the floor, and checked her phone for the first time in hours.

One text, from Brett. What time are you home tonight?

It was from a couple of hours ago, and he was probably already in bed. The subtext read, "You're going to wake me up, aren't you? I need my beauty sleep. I'm a powerful lawyer."

Okay, that was a bitchy interpretation, but she had the spirit of it pegged.

She tapped out, Not sure. Late. and shut the thing off. Suddenly wiped, she was tempted to contradict the message and head for the subway. Who knew how long Mercer would need to stay?

Then her mood shifted, weariness gone in a breath as silly, glittery excitement burst inside her like confetti.

She had a second to register Rich's haughty, blinding smile before he was swarmed by a dozen well-wishers and autograph-seeking kids, Lindsey's view blocked. Thank goodness, too. The drinks had her feeling loose, and she could use a minute to pull herself together.

Rich was a ridiculously good-looking man. Scary-sexy with his shirt off, and devastating in a suit. His gorgeous, masculine face, dark eyes and shoulder-length black hair had earned him his fight nickname. Broad shoulders and chest, slim waist, then those hips and that butt and those thighs and…ooh, tremble. His shape seemed made-up, like the heroes in those comic books Brett used to care so much about.

Rich could've easily skewed toward being *too* perfect, except for that accent, peppered with swearwords and strong enough to strip the wax out of your ears. It all worked great as a swaggering ring persona, but his over-the-topness wasn't an act, Lindsey didn't think, and that was enough to keep smart girls from getting any reckless romantic notions about the man. Though it didn't keep her body from wanting his.

Lust object? *Go for it.* But she held herself back from slapping a few other labels on Rich. Rebound material? *In your dreams, Tuttle.*

Still, as the crowd thinned and her view of him cleared,

she felt her pulse race, hormones elbowing her better judgment aside.

Six feet, three inches of good-sense-wrecking kryptonite. And if Lindsey were her own client, she wouldn't be letting herself anywhere near Rich Estrada.

2

BUT INADVISABLE NEARNESS was exactly what Lindsey got only a moment later.

Rich escaped the crowd, heading in her direction. He blinked in recognition and surprise, and blinded her with that lethal smile.

"Look who it is." Stopping in front of her, he slipped the suit jacket from his shoulders. The space was stuffy. He hadn't worn a tie, but he undid an extra button on his dress shirt. "Almost didn't recognize you outside that office."

"Hello, Mr. Champion. Well done." She hazarded a clap on his arm then regretted it, now knowing exactly how hard that particular body part was. As if she needed another thing to fixate on.

Rich shrugged, uncharacteristically humble. "Just a regional title. I'm still in the minors."

"For now."

He tossed his jacket on the radiator. "Thanks for coming. And for sticking around this long."

"Hey, free drinks."

Rich laughed.

"It was fun. My pleasure."

He sighed, a tired, genuine noise, and took a seat beside

her—though not quite as close as Lindsey would have preferred. She'd never seen him like this. So…accessible. Probably just exhausted. He flirted with her every chance he got, and not subtly. As though it was a sport, one he played with every woman he came across.

He rolled his sleeves up to his elbows, forearms flexing with tendons and making Lindsey's brain glaze over.

"You actually watch any, or was it too gory?"

"Oh, no, I watched the whole thing."

"It's an acquired taste."

"Then I just may have acquired it tonight." Oops—was that a flirty smirk she'd felt pass her lips? *Quit thinking so hard. He's just the obnoxious, sexy guy from the gym downstairs.* The one she'd developed an extremely troubling fascination with the past couple weeks. Probably some self-defeating relationship-sabotage crush. Naughty matchmaker.

A server came through with a tray of champagne flutes. Rich snagged two, handing one to Lindsey.

"Thanks. Cheers to your big win."

They clinked. His dark eyes held hers as he drank. Goddamn, she could fall into that stare and drown, grinning as the world went black.

"How come your face isn't all screwed up?" she blurted.

Rich laughed, a deep and far too exciting noise.

"No, really. Haven't you ever had your nose broken?"

"Sure. Twice. And what about all this?" He pointed to a couple scratches and the bandage, and the stitched gash nearly healed beside it. She'd dabbed concealer on that once—long story. Been close enough to smell his skin, as she could now. Tonight that scent tried to hide behind a hint of cologne, but she found it easily, breathed it in.

She pulled herself together and waved dismissively. "Surface stuff. I get those shaving my legs. How come you're not… You know."

"More like Merce?"

Lindsey wouldn't say Mercer was unattractive, but he looked, perfectly aptly, like a man who'd spent the past decade getting routinely punched in the face. Whereas Rich…

"You're too pretty," Lindsey concluded. "Too symmetrical. And your ears aren't hideous enough."

He smiled, looking away as though she'd actually managed to make this shameless man bashful. She took the opportunity to ogle his forearm again, and the way his dress shirt pulled taut against his locked biceps.

Their eyes met once more. "You implying I'm doing my job wrong?" he asked between sips. "Seems like letting my face get scrambled as little as possible would be to my credit."

"Fair enough. Are you happy with how you did tonight?"

"You actually wanna hear the long, incredibly boring answer to that?"

"Sure."

"I'm happy I won," Rich said, swirling his champagne so the foam rose. "And I know the way it happened will be great for lining up another match, to prove I didn't just stumble into a title with a lucky punch. If Higgins and I ever wind up in the same pro organization, I'll probably get a nice rematch, maybe even move up the card, if they spin this into some rivalry. But I would've liked a bit more of a tangle with that asshole."

Lindsey nursed her drink as he recounted the details, asking questions when she didn't understand a term.

He laughed after ten minutes' conversational dominance. "You fake not being bored really well. Tell me to shut up anytime."

"I don't mind. We *are* at a fight, after all."

"True."

"Are you what they call a technical fighter?" She'd heard

the term someplace, and it now accounted for a healthy percentage of her meager MMA vocabulary.

Rich shook his head. "Mercer's a technical fighter. Means he can execute a kick or punch with, like, robotic precision. Me, I'm sloppier, but when I hit, no matter how busted it might be, I like it to land hard. Like, *hard*. Plus I'm not the strongest grappler. Best if I can mess a guy up while we're still standing. I do what they call sprawl-and-brawl, avoid going down to the mat whenever possible."

She crossed her legs, accidentally brushing Rich's shin with her bare foot. *Zing.* She cleared her throat. "Sorry. So, how did you get into all this? Tell me you were in med school or something, then you had a nervous breakdown and went all *Fight Club.*"

He cocked a skeptical brow. "You wish I was a doctor?"

"No, I mean, it'd be cool if you had some upstanding life before you went rogue. It's such a romantic cliché," she said with a silly sigh. Oops, that'd be the champagne.

"Sorry, I was never upstanding. Grew up poor, immigrant parents, got in tons of fights in grade school. High school dropout. But I could lie, if it gets you all worked up."

Lindsey grinned, hoping her blush didn't show. "Nah."

"You sure? What do you want me to be, in my previous life? Investment banker? Oil magnate?"

She laughed.

"Lawyer?"

"Definitely not," she said a bit too passionately.

He bumped her shoulder with his. "Disgraced royalty?"

"That would explain your fight name."

"Nah, that's just because of my aforementioned pretty face," he said, flashing her a smile worthy of an Armani campaign.

"It's the nose. You have a very princely nose." She nearly reached up to touch said nose, but perhaps mercifully, Jenna and Mercer wandered over. Lindsey edged herself farther from Rich's hip. Assuring Jenna she was freshly single in front of him seemed lacking in both class and subtlety.

Jenna beckoned Rich to his feet for a hug. "I wondered where you were hiding. Congratulations. If I'd been able to bring myself to watch, I'd say you looked great."

"I always look great." Rich and Mercer gave each other the standard manly half-hug-slash-handshake.

"Great work, man," Mercer said. "Just don't forget where you came from, once you sign with an org."

"I'm sure I won't, not with the Wilinski's branding you'll want plastered all over my shorts."

"We're about ready to head out. Did you still want to catch a ride with us?" Jenna asked Lindsey just as someone came around refreshing the champagne.

"Oh…" She watched the foam rise in her glass. She didn't want to leave yet. She wanted to stay and keep flirting with Rich, keep this lovely buzz stoked and put off getting bitched at by Brett for waking him up. But the subway would stop running shortly and cabs were expensive, especially if she was soon likely to be on her own, paying rent…. "I guess I should."

"Where do you live?" Rich asked.

"Brigham Circle."

"You can share my cab later."

"You sure?"

"Sure I'm sure. It's on the promotion company's dime."

"Okay. Great." Far better than great.

"Right," Jenna said, giving Lindsey a *look,* one she translated to mean *Don't forget you have a man at home* or some similarly fretful matchmaker admonishment. "I'll see you Monday. Have a great weekend, both of you."

Lindsey watched them disappear into the chaos, suddenly

shy now that her evening was officially slated to end in the same vehicle as Prince Richard.

"Wait." She turned to him as he sat. "Don't you live in Lynn? Isn't that, like, twenty miles from where I am? In the opposite direction?"

"Like I said—not my fare to pay."

She smiled, tapping his glass with hers. "Any plans for your prize money?"

"Help my mom out with some bills, get my car fixed. Nothing flashy."

"Saving those flashy plans for when you're one of the main event guys?" She shook her head, boggled by the top-level payouts. "Fifty grand for a night's work."

"I know. Still, nothing compared to Tyson back in the day, or the big Vegas boxing matches. Seven figures for a single fight."

She looked him in the eye, feeling a flash of intimacy and praying it didn't show on her face. "Think you'll ever be that big? A million dollars big?"

"Nah. Even for the biggest events in UFC, the main event guys don't take home more than two or three hundred grand. And those are the *top* Ultimate Fighting Championship guys. Celebrity types. Names you might actually recognize outside the sport. People are only just realizing it's not a fad or some pro-wrestling-type sideshow."

Lindsey tried to imagine any woman seeing a commercial featuring a half-naked Rich and not finding herself turned on. To the sport. Turned on to the sport. "I should buy shares."

"I'll buy shares in Spark, then. Mercer says your stable of singletons is growing nicely."

"I'm meeting with my first client on Thursday." Sort of. She'd be shadowing and assisting Jenna to start, completing a couple courses this fall before being officially cleared to oversee her own clients. "And you'll be on the road soon—no longer a threat to the female population of Spark."

"Their loss." His gaze shifted to some distraction in the middle distance.

"Are you looking forward to whatever's next? Jetting off to exotic foreign locales?"

His eyes met hers once more. Goodness, they were dark. And deep. Boring through her skull and dismantling her good sense.

"No jets for me," Rich said. "More like motor lodges off the freeway or somebody's spare room near whatever facility my future manager sends me to train at."

"But you *are* leaving Wilinski's, right?"

Word came down the corridor that people were relocating to a club. Rich nodded his comprehension but turned back to Lindsey.

"I'll get sent away to some camp for a while, so I'll have a chance to try on the competition." He looked thoughtful a moment.

"What?"

Rich's voice went quiet, nearly soft, and he dropped his gaze to the glass in Lindsey's hand. "It feels shitty, saying that. Like I've outgrown the gym."

"Maybe you have."

"I've been making do with what I got for as long as I've been alive. Wilinski's is my style—scrappy and broke." He frowned. "We could make it a lot more than what it is, if we had the money."

"How do you get money? More members?"

"Yeah."

"And how do you get more members? By producing big-name fighters, right?"

"That's a good way."

"Then all you have to do is go out there and set the world on fire, Rich."

He smiled, though the gesture drooped with melancholy. "There's a part of me that's afraid I'll go off, train for a few months in some state-of-the-art facility and forget where I came from."

She was peeking through the slimmest crack in his shell, offered a glimpse of a man who wasn't as cocksure as he liked everyone to believe.

"That's your choice to make, I suppose." Emotion and alcohol had her reaching out and rubbing his arm, patting his shoulder. The contact was intense, a mix of intimacy and awe at the sheer hardness of him. She took her hand back, feeling drunk.

For a moment their eyes met, then Rich dropped his gaze. "Sorry to unload. It's been a hell of a day."

"I'll bet. You going to the club?"

"Nah, I've had enough excitement for one night. Plus I gotta be in the gym at ten."

"Jeez, no rest for the wicked."

"You wanna get out of here? Must be pushing two."

Get out of there and go home *alone?* Or together? The exhaustion was gone from his eyes, replaced with his usual mischief, if she wasn't mistaken. "Sure."

He stood, stooping for her shoes and sliding them onto her feet. Lindsey blushed to the roots of her hair and stammered a thank-you.

Rich stopped by the locker room for his gym bag, and Lindsey carried his jacket. The weight of it felt peculiar, draped over her arm. Personal. She wanted to put her nose to the collar and find his smell there. She wanted to pretend she'd forgotten she was holding it when they got to her place so she could keep it. But that was lame and a little creepy, and an invitation for uncomfortable questions from Brett.

Stupid crush, making her all crazy.

The night air was enlivening, and Lindsey suddenly felt wide-awake. She wished for a dozen things in a breath—for Rich's arm around her shoulders or his hand claiming hers, for a hot, loaded look or a brazen invitation. The only gesture she got was the simple opening of her door when he selected a cab from the curbside lineup. Her heart beat in her throat for the few seconds it took him to stow his bag and circle to the other side.

He seemed impossibly big as he settled beside her.

She gave the driver her address. It was only a fifteen-minute ride, this time of night. The backseat felt strange after the arena, so quiet and close. She glanced Rich's way. "Did you meet any managers you liked?"

"Two or three I thought I could stand working with. Got their cards, so I'll have to do some research this week and make my pick."

"If you get your rematch, I'll be sure to come."

"Excellent. My first official groupie."

"You wish. What if I show up in my Greg the Trucker shirt?"

Rich winced. "If that dirtbag's your type, I am *not* sharing a cab with you."

"Just kidding. And fine, I'll be your groupie. Just don't think you get to sign my cleavage."

He laughed, eyes squinching in a way that seemed to double his sex appeal.

Not wanting their rapport to end, Lindsey asked a couple more questions about the sport. Rich answered, then added, "You really got some bloodlust in you."

"No, it's not that." An image flashed—his hips, his thighs, his sweat-gleaming stomach and incredible arms. "Some different kind of primal something-or-other. Did you have any family watching tonight?"

"Nah. My mom thinks it's barbaric—she grew up in Colombia, in a real rough area. She's seen more than enough fighting for anybody's lifetime. And my sister gets too stressed out."

"You really love it, huh?" What was it like, to be so passionate about something? Lindsey thought she was reasonably driven, but she wouldn't say wedding planning and matchmaking were her callings. Careers, perhaps, and satisfying ones, but not passions. Maybe she just wasn't passionate. Not the way Rich was.

"I do love it," he said. "It's all I know, really. Gotta milk it for all it's worth while I'm still in good shape. Maybe in ten years I'll have to think about earning something flashier than a GED and find a respectable gig."

"You could coach."

He shook his head. "I'd rather see guys as opponents than students. I'll leave all that nurturing bull to Mercer."

"Well, your immediate future looks awfully bright. Let's hope they'll be able to understand your accent, wherever you wind up."

"Tease all you want—you'll miss me when I'm gone." He said it through a self-satisfied sigh.

"I'm sure I'll get more work done without you sticking your princely nose around the office door every ten minutes."

"How come you never say yes when I ask if you wanna grab lunch?"

Lindsey's face heated in the darkness. "I'm always busy when you ask." In truth she'd said no because often she and Brett were on-again, or because Rich flat-out intimidated her. It wasn't as though she floated through her workday on a champagne cloud of boldness. On a good day Lindsey suspected she was cute, but Rich was *stunning*. Men like that didn't simply stroll around with passably cute girls. She'd spent enough time feeling invisible. The next time she got into a romance with somebody, she wanted a man she could shine beside, and Rich was too bright to do anything but cast others in his shadow.

"Maybe now that I'm leaving," he said, "you'll deign to say yes, just once. Take pity on a man."

"We'll see."

"I don't like the sound of that. What about after work? Jenna must let you go home at some point. Long enough to get a drink down the street?"

Her blush burned hotter than ever. "Are you asking me on a date?"

"Say yes and find out."

She glanced out the window, champagne courage abandoning her. Dammit, why did she have to clam up at moments like this? But for once, her mouth sided with her body. "Okay."

"Yeah?"

"Yes. Okay."

Rich shook his fist in triumph. "Nice. Frigging finally."

She laughed. "I hesitate to fuel your already turbocharged ego. But yes, fine. I'll go out for a drink with you some evening after work."

For a long moment they didn't speak. Rich's darting eyes seemed to watch her with some sly persuasion of fondness, as though she amused and baffled him equally. Must be a rarity for him—a woman who didn't visibly melt into a puddle in his presence. Thank goodness he didn't know how wobbly he made her knees, simply passing by her office.

Her gaze snagged on his mouth, on the sexiest set of lips she'd ever seen. Always ready with a smirk or a curse-riddled diatribe. She wondered what else they might offer.

She was staring. They were both staring, though the pointedness of it didn't seem to unnerve Rich a jot. Then again, he routinely peered into the eyes of men hell-bent on knocking him unconscious.

"What?" she asked, unable to bear the suspense.

"I dunno. Were we about to kiss?"

Her heart pounded. "Oh. I didn't think we were. I was just staring because you were staring."

"I was waiting for some little female signal. But your poker face is stone-cold."

Kiss me, she wanted to say. *Tackle me.* Rich was too much for her to get hung up on, but for a fling? For some fun in the back of a cab? Not her type, but so exciting. So unlike any man she'd ever experienced. Not that there'd been many.

Without her willing them to, Lindsey's lips parted. And it was all the invitation he needed.

His hand was at her neck, strong and warm, and as he ran his thumb along her jaw, she felt sparks prickling. He lowered his face to hers, noses touching first, then mouths.

It was as though she'd never done this before. He felt so new, so different after all those years with the same man. Heat pooled in her cheeks, her chest, between her legs.

They twisted in their spots, hands seeking faces, seat belts binding laps. Rich tilted his head, parted lips asking to take this kiss deeper.

His mouth grew hungrier, tongue seeking hers. She found his collar clutched in her hand, no clue how it had happened. His kisses made Lindsey's head swim, made her most scandalous exploits seem a chaste hand-holding. What on earth would *sex* with this man be like?

Ooh, terrible thought. Terrible, brilliant thought.

He broke them apart to murmur, "I've been wondering for weeks what you taste like." He freed the buckle of his seat belt and slid beside her.

Lust folded in on itself, desire making her entire body tight and hot and angry. His hand was warm and broad, thumb on her cheek, fingers fanned possessively over her jaw.

She stroked his chest through his shirt, touched his face,

fascinated by his soft skin, rough stubble, the texture of his bandage and the edge of the cut it hid. Maleness personified, an entirely new species.

His mouth was perfect—pushy, masterful, sinful. His hands felt so good on her neck and shoulder…how amazing would they feel elsewhere?

Just as her mind began to wander, she felt a funny sensation at her hip, a tingling that wasn't in any way erotic. She wrested her lips from his.

"Is that your phone?"

"Just a text. Like I care."

His mouth was on hers again, hungry and impolite. How long since she'd been kissed this way? Ages and ages and ages. Maybe never. She grasped his shirt, crisp cotton in her fist, hard muscle under her knuckles. He had to hunch to keep their mouths on par, seeming so big and looming and wrong and awesome she wanted to claw him.

Another intrusion from his phone—a nagging ping.

"Maybe it's a manager," she teased, lips still pressed to his. "They want you so badly, they're texting at 3:00 a.m."

"Probably some drunk friend. They'll call if it's important." He took her mouth.

No one's kissing had ever done this to her before, made her so hot she could feel herself getting wet. Just from *kissing.*

But again, a ping had her pulling away.

Rich sighed. "Hang on. This is going to drive me up a frigging wall." He checked the screen, face lit white. "It's Mercer." He hit a button, eyes darting, brows pulling together in a frown. After a few seconds he turned his phone off.

"Everything okay?"

Rich blinked, gaze focused past her, out the window. "Yeah, yeah. Everything's fine."

Whatever the urgent bro-message had been, it killed their

make-out session dead. Rich shifted back to his side and buckled his seat belt with a cold snap.

Her heart sank.

At least this fixed her worries about seeming rude by not inviting him up. Though it would've been nice for the kiss to end under duress, at her curb, all fraught with both of them wishing it could continue in somebody's bed. She'd have ended it, been the one to seemingly muster self-control, since there was no way she'd have told him it was because her ex was upstairs. She could have—*should* have—left this unflappable man all flustered and won this round of their little sexual-tension battle.

"This is me," she said as they reached her building. She forced a smile, hoping she looked unaffected to have lost his attention to a text, and so suddenly. The greatest make-out session of her life, clearly just a whim in Rich's estimations.

"Thanks again for coming out." He laid a perfectly, *horribly* chaste kiss on her cheek.

"Oh, sure." She folded his jacket on the seat between them.

"Take care."

"You, too."

And with a thank-you to the driver, she was on the sidewalk. Rich waved her toward the building and she heard the cab pull away once she made it safely into the foyer.

Her legs were lead as she headed up the steps, and she was halfway to her apartment when she realized it.

The most obvious answer was usually the correct one, and the most obvious answer was that it hadn't been Mercer who'd texted, but some girlfriend Rich had neglected to mention. Or, equally gutting, a better offer for a night's recreation.

And just like that, her sails went limp. Just like that, she realized she'd been a fool to think she might be anything more to him than a convenient female body.

She entered her apartment, and as she closed the door, she

wasn't just shutting it on the hallway or the October chill. She shut it on her gullible heart and her weak body, for having made her lose track of her head, if only for a night.

3

Ten months later

RICH FOLLOWED THE GREETER to a booth with an underwhelming view of the diner's parking lot. He had to remind himself where he even was, the travel had taken such a toll.

Albuquerque. Last week of July. Day before the event he'd been living and breathing for the past eight weeks. Fight night.

Just another match. No big deal. He had to keep thinking that, but in truth it was the chance of a lifetime, like tripping over a pot of gold.

Something about Rich—his personality, no doubt—had rubbed Nick Moreau, the current light heavyweight champ, the wrong way. Rich had responded in kind when asked what he thought of Moreau, and a flame war had caught fire, a back-and-forth Rich had hoped might one day land him a well-publicized grudge match. But when Moreau's opponent for the big event had fractured a rib in May, the champ had a ready suggestion. "Gimme Estrada. I'll shut that pretty—*bleep*—'s mouth for him once and for all."

A stab at the frigging light heavyweight belt, not even a year after signing. That was *nuts*.

And to think he'd earned the chance just by being unbearably obnoxious!

The waitress came by, but Rich didn't need the menu.

"Four egg whites, scrambled, no salt, and four pieces of dry wheat toast."

She scribbled on her pad.

"And a glass of skim milk and a piece of whatever fruit you got."

"Banana okay? Anything else you can only get in pie form."

If only. "Banana's perfect."

She departed along with the laminated sheet showcasing whatever deliciousness Rich was missing out on. At least tonight he'd get a steak. A lean, unsalted steak and a side of equally undoctored steamed vegetables.

Still, the weigh-in would be done the next morning, the fight that evening. Then it'd take a team of horses to keep him off the nearest plate of ribs.

When his breakfast arrived, Rich tried to overlay the image of his mother's *bandeja paisa,* an obscene Colombian orgy of a meal. Beans, dirty rice, pork, more pork, plantain, avocado, yet more pork… He'd think of these rubbery, tasteless egg whites when he landed his first kick, this sickly, bluish so-called milk when he caught the guy with an elbow. He'd dedicate the fight to the god of fatty, rare steaks and strong beer, and he'd earn himself a knockout, no question.

It was nice to have an hour away from Chris. His manager was a schmoozy weenie, but apparently schmoozing worked—look where it had landed Rich. But he wasn't an ace at being told what to do. Chris was busy with prefight stuff that morning, leaving Rich free to enjoy his solitude. Trouble was, whenever he had a little solitude, his brain filled the space with distraction. A sort of five-foot-six-ish distraction, with dark blond hair and insanely blue eyes, freckles and a wry half smile.

That always happened when Rich had his sights set on a girl but hadn't gotten with her yet. He fixated. Like the ribs, he hungered for what he couldn't have. Or rather, what he'd chosen *not* to have, because she'd made him pretty certain in the back of that cab, he could've had her.

Then he'd gotten the text from Mercer's number.

Before you get any ideas, champ, you should probably know Lindsey's got a live-in boyfriend. —Jenna

Yeah, he should have known that. Too bad Lindsey hadn't been the one to inform him of it.

Jesus, nearly ten months ago that had happened, and he was still hung up. It made no sense, but he could remember her face better than that of the last woman he'd woken next to, only a few days ago. The road must be making him crazy. Or Lindsey made him crazy. She certainly had that night after the fight—not just the messing around, but the way he opened his mouth when her eyes were on him and...*stuff* just came out. Stuff he never shared with people, except maybe his mom and sister. Emotions and crap.

The waitress came by. "Anything else?"

"Just the check."

She tore the item in question from a pad and set it on the table.

"Thank the cook for accommodating my ridiculous eggs," he said with a smile.

"We've been getting lots of weird requests. You must be with the...sorry, I've forgotten what it's called. The kick-boxing thing."

"I'm sure we'll drive you all crazy tonight, ordering

chicken breasts with no skin or oil or salt. Worse than a bunch of supermodels before a runway show."

She smiled at that, and Rich tried to imagine her naked, just to see if the image banished Lindsey's smirking face from his head. No such luck. The waitress wandered off, but the only backside preoccupying him was two thousand miles away, for better or worse.

Definitely worse.

Rich wasn't a saint by anyone's standards, but it had stung, discovering he'd made out with another man's woman. His younger self wouldn't have thought twice about it, but he was older and wiser and generally less of a self-centered dick. Even if he didn't feel an obligation to the poor jerk— probably out of town on a business trip or something—he had the pride to think he deserved the attentions of a woman decent enough not to cheat on someone.

Weird, though. Lindsey had seemed so like the opposite of that kind of woman. No time for B.S. Hell, the girl was a matchmaker.

Still, none of it kept him from imagining everything he'd opted out of.

He wouldn't be back in Boston until Christmas, once the last of his three contracted fights wrapped in Cleveland. Three matches in the big leagues in less than a year. Hell of a run. But it was also a hell of an opportunity, and he was in freaky-good shape. If lightning struck, he'd win tomorrow, earn himself a title no one expected him to, and hopefully get to drop that December bout in favor of something a bit further out, maybe even a main event. Even if he lost, he could sleep easy knowing where the cash was coming from to pay his mom's hospital bills. Knowing there were no financial clouds looming while she recovered from her heart valve replacement… Though it stung that he hadn't been there to hold her hand. He'd been training, as always, cuffed to his coaches in the run-up to his April match in Vancouver.

It was a stroke of astounding good fortune that he was good enough at what he loved to support his family doing it, and to be a viable age when MMA had all this commercial steam. The chance to make up for everything his father had fallen short on.

Rich's father had been a small man, in both stature and character. He'd been crippled by a depression Rich had found alternately heartbreaking and infuriating. He knew the depression had come about because the man mourned his homeland, his culture, his identity. But that didn't make it okay.

Rich's sympathy had run out at puberty. He'd gotten lucky, though, and stumbled into boxing, a pastime built for seething young men looking for the next best thing to hauling off and punching their fathers in the face.

Now he was twenty-nine—a little old to just be breaking out, but he had a hotter fire under his ass than plenty of these twenty-four-year-olds, and no ego aside from the act he put on for the audience and acquaintances, for everyone but his mother and younger sister. Strip all that bravado away, leave Rich alone with himself—here in this restaurant, in fact— and he felt like little more than a dog. A tough, loyal dog, alternately protective and savage.

It left no room for a life outside the ring and the bonds of his family, but in no time at all, he'd wake up and find he was thirty-five, thirty-six, thirty-seven…past his prime, shunted to the backseat to train or manage younger prospects. A worthy and important role, but one Rich wouldn't ever take to without bitterness, not the way Mercer had. But he still had five good years or more, hopefully enough to banish the Estradas' financial worries for good, so his mom could quit giving herself Catholic guilt fits every time she needed a procedure to keep her heart beating.

Every time she cried, another patch of Rich's heart turned black toward his father, another vertebra calcified, rock-hard, steeling his determination that he'd never be like his dad. Better a strong, dumb dog than a weak, cowering ghost.

He tossed his banana peel onto the plate, fished out some bills and weighted them down with the otherwise neglected saltshaker.

Back to the grind. Back to the routines that kept this body sore and brain quiet, kept his mind off his anger and worry. Kept his muscles taxed and his energy spent, too beat to succumb to any distracting thoughts about Lindsey at night, in whatever anonymous motel room he called his kennel that week.

"Oh, shut up! It's starting." Lindsey waved her hands, shushing Brett and Jenna's conversation about…whatever they'd been talking about. She cranked the volume as the pay-per-view coverage began, heart thumping in her throat.

The announcer ran down the event's matchups, and she whooped along with Jenna when head shots of Rich and his opponent slid in from either side of the screen, their stats appearing beneath them.

"Wow," Jenna said. "Second-to-last fight. What a difference a few months make."

Nine months and three weeks, to be precise, since that fight in Boston. And yeah, a lot had changed.

Jenna was engaged. Mercer had won the money to buy her a ring back in the spring, his first paid boxing match in years. Seemed fast to Lindsey, but the two had been living together since the week they'd met. At this clip, Jenna would be pregnant with twins by Halloween.

Lindsey, on the other hand, was still thoroughly *not* engaged. So not engaged, in fact, that she and Brett were officially over, even if they'd agreed to share the apartment until

Lindsey found a new place she could afford. And in this college town, that wasn't likely until September rolled around. Five weeks was a long time to cohabit with your ex, civil though things were.

At least work was good. Her own relationship might be over, but she could still drum up enthusiasm for other people's, and she seemed to be pretty adept at matchmaking. A few of her clients were pains in the butt, but on the whole, she looked forward to going to work. Though some of that could be attributed to her desire to escape her awkward living situation.

Brett stood. "Anything from the kitchen?"

Lindsey handed him her empty beer bottle. "Thanks. And thank *you* for coming over," she added to Jenna. "I would've thought you'd had it up to your eyeballs with fighting by now."

"I have to see if Rich wins, live and in color."

Lindsey nodded, filled as ever by a stupid rush of bad-girlfriend adrenaline at the mention of his name. Though she wasn't anybody's girlfriend now.

"And a night out is nice," Jenna said. "Beats watching at Hooters with the guys from the gym and all that testosterone. You've certainly gotten into all this—enough to shell out to watch."

"Oh, yeah," Brett said, returning to the couch with two bottles. "You should see Lindsey's porn stash."

She rolled her eyes as Jenna's widened.

Brett passed Lindsey her beer then leaned over to pull open the side table drawer. He plopped a few glossy MMA magazines in Jenna's lap.

"I see." Jenna flipped one open, then immediately winced at a photo of a freeze-framed punch.

Lindsey nearly distracted her by mentioning Rich was in that issue, then stopped herself. Best not reveal to either of her couch mates that she knew which page he was on.

Her embarrassment preempted as the first match began, Lindsey took the magazines back, leaned over Brett and shut them in the drawer.

This event had cost her fifty bucks to order—fifty bucks that should probably have been put toward a security deposit or moving van rental. She ought to be absorbing every second of it, but all she could concentrate on was the clock, and how soon Rich's fight would be starting.

Her crush was ridiculous. And harmless? Now, perhaps. But she had to admit, it may have contributed to her permanently breaking up with Brett. It wasn't as though she'd thought about Rich while she'd been kissing Brett or anything heinous…but she did occasionally space out on the subway, lost in the memory of those minutes in the back of that cab.

Stupid girl. For all she knew, she'd kissed some other woman's lover.

Whatever the case, they'd never gone out for that drink. And Rich hadn't been back to Wilinski's more than twice in the past six months, too busy training in California. She'd seen him during those visits, but they'd exchanged only passing pleasantries, nothing that indicated they'd shared anything special. Not that they'd been alone and in any position to flirt, but still—there hadn't been any of that old fire in his eye contact. Something cagey, she'd thought, something more than she'd find in a friend's gaze, but no hot promises, none of the heat she'd glimpsed that night in October, the wickedness she'd assumed came standard with Rich Estrada.

The opening matches went on forever. She knew a few of the names, enough to have favorites to root for, but she was too antsy to concentrate.

"Popcorn?" she asked Brett and Jenna, not waiting for an answer.

As she stripped the cellophane from the packet in the kitchen, she commanded her heart to slow. For the entire three and a half minutes the popcorn bag twirled in the micro-wave, she counted her breaths. How dumb, to get this wound up over seeing some man she *kind of* knew on TV.

Why should her heart hurt this way? Well, probably be-cause she'd been stalking his career for long enough to ges-tate a baby.

Yeah, *stalking*—she could admit it. She wasn't alone in her admiration, only alone in denying it. Rich had a bona fide fan base, a digital harem of noisy groupies who called themselves the Courtesans and swooned about him in tact-less, filthy detail on message boards.

Did they go to the events? Follow his fights in person from city to city, not just on-screen? Did they toss themselves at him after the matches, and if so, did he like that? Was his hotel bed warmed by some new admirer every night?

And most important, why should she even frigging care?

She sighed as the microwave beeped, frustrated to the bone. With herself, for having gotten so hung up. With her living situation, and for what was surely going to prove the longest August in history. And from a phone call she'd got-ten earlier—her mother calling to say Lindsey's youngest sister, Maya, was threatening to not go back to high school in September for her senior year. Lindsey had promised to talk some sense into her this weekend. As always, the peace-keeper mitigating others' drama.

Yet even with all that on her mind, her thoughts wandered back to Rich. His face and mouth, those fingers on her neck. Whatever she felt, it was no glimmer, no silly stirring. It was infatuation like she'd never suffered before, made all the worse by the way they'd parted. Some nights she was tempted to demand his number from Mercer, drink half a bottle of wine and text him, What the heck was in that message that made you stop kissing me?

But for all she knew, the reply she'd get would be, We kissed? When was that? Lindsey who?

She carried the popcorn and a roll of paper towels back through to the living room and settled between her ex-boyfriend and her boss.

"Nearly time," Jenna said, sitting on the edge of the cushion with her knuckles pressed to her lips. "Oh, God, I hate this stupid sport."

Brett took over the popcorn, which was just as well. As soon as the announcers began discussing Rich's match, Lindsey felt sick.

"Should be a close one," the first announcer said. "Estrada's been on his game, but can that stack up against Moreau's experience?"

"It's going to come down to who's hungrier for it," a second announcer declared. "Though the odds in Vegas say Moreau's belt won't be going anywhere tonight."

The screen flashed to backstage prep, to Nick Moreau jogging in place. He was good—a mean-looking thirtysomething from Quebec with a shaved head, a bit of a veteran. Then to Rich, and Lindsey's heart stopped. A close-up of that handsome profile, his expression stern and set. He stretched his neck and licked his lips, then suddenly he was moving, the camera swiveling to follow as he was ushered through double doors into the dark arena.

"Oh, God, oh, God," Jenna muttered.

Rich's cocky, regal shtick hadn't changed. He walked down the aisle to the same music, welcomed with a mix of cheers and boos as his stats were announced. He was extremely popular with Hispanic fans—and with any woman possessed of eyes and a pulse—but hated by his fair share of enthusiasts, too.

Moreau strode out to some hard-core rock song, minimalist in black warm-ups, his scalp gleaming under the lights.

Lindsey felt a pain in her palm and realized she was clenching her fist hard enough to leave nail marks.

The fighters had stripped to their shorts and gloves, both hopping and jogging in place, keeping warm. Rich shook out his arms and tossed punches in the air.

The announcer went through the rigmarole, rattling through the rules for the three-round match, and the men went back to their corners. A ring girl circled, and with a shout, the fight was on.

"Oh, God," Jenna said again. If the throw pillow in her lap had been an animal, she'd already have crushed the life out of it.

Lindsey held her breath and bit her lip, hands squished between her clenched thighs.

Rich took the offensive early. Moreau was a more cautious, strategic fighter. Rich baited him with a few quick swipes, but Moreau waited for an opening.

"Oh!" Jenna cried when the first punch landed. It was a soft, harmless jab to Rich's shoulder, but she buried her face in the pillow all the same. Lindsey teetered at the edge of the cushion.

The two fighters clinched for a few seconds, each landing a couple of good shots.

"Stay on your feet," Lindsey murmured. "Stay on your feet." Moreau was good on the mat—a far stronger grappler, even after Rich's past months of world-class training. Or so she'd read in one of her incriminating magazines.

Rich knocked his opponent with a sharp hook then dodged aside, clearly content to keep this fight upright.

"Good. Good." How had Mercer survived being in Rich's and Delante's corners? Lindsey felt a heart attack brewing just watching from the other side of the country. Yet she could practically feel everything, live and in three dimensions. Hear the crowd all around her as she had at the Boston fight, smell the sweat and feel the heat of the lights and bodies.

"Estrada's come out strong," the first announcer observed. "But Moreau's known for his pacing." True.

"Be cool," she muttered. "Save something for the other two rounds."

"I have no idea who's winning," Brett said.

"No one yet."

By the time the horn blared to end the round, the two men had had a good dance, but neither was the clear favorite. Lindsey shoved popcorn in her face, just to have something to do.

Jenna peeked from behind her pillow. "What happened?"

"They're both holding steady," Lindsey said.

Jenna went back into hiding the second the ring girl was done prancing.

Lindsey didn't know what Moreau's trainer had said to him during the break, but he came out with a fire under his ass, going right for Rich's legs. *Get him on his back.* That's what he'd been told.

Rich dodged Moreau's efforts to kick his feet out from under him, and with a solid roundhouse to the ribs he sent the other man stumbling into the chain-link.

"Yes," Lindsey groaned, hugging the bowl. Her heart punched her ribs with every beat, easily a million times a minute.

Rich sneaked in a flurry of jabs, then took a mean hit to the ear. He gave twice as good as he got, banging Moreau in the ribs with his knee. Thirty seconds before the horn, Moreau hooked him behind the legs and got them onto the ground, but they ended the round in a mutual tangle, neither in danger of submitting. Lindsey gulped a breath when the air horn sounded, the first she'd taken since the fighters had hit the mat.

"Anything?" Jenna asked from behind her pillow.

"Nothing deciding." But Moreau was probably winning now, if this fight came down to points.

"If Moreau can manage that again, early in the third," noted the announcer, "we might just have a match on our hands."

"He better not!"

"Linds." Brett zapped her a look, the kind you'd send your kid when they lost track of their indoor voice. She shot one back, feeling no need to be ladylike, given the occasion. Especially considering how noisy Brett got whenever the Pats played the Giants.

The third round started. Moreau had gotten a taste for dominating and wanted more. He was going for Rich's legs, looking to get them back to the mat. Before he could, Rich seized an opening, landing a half dozen serious head shots and taking only a single nasty hook to the cheek. There was blood beside Moreau's mouth, more of the same slicking Rich's curled fingers.

"Jesus," Brett muttered, clearly missing the civility of football.

Then, disaster.

Moreau bent low and caught Rich behind his knee. Rich retaliated with an elbow between Moreau's shoulder blades and wormed his way out of the clinch. They traded jabs, then Rich nearly snagged an opening, missing Moreau's ribs with a roundhouse kick but still banging his arm, and hard. Something had happened—the crowd's collective voice flared in a passionate ruckus, but Lindsey didn't know why. Had that kick been illegal?

"That's not good," the announcer said.

She straightened. "What's not good? For who?"

Then something strange happened. After a moment of staggered circling and punching, Moreau lunged, looking to take Rich down. And Rich seemed to let him.

She shot to her feet, popcorn jumping from the bowl. "No!"

The men tumbled to the ground, scrambling for position before they even hit the mat. Moreau came out on top and landed three brutal punches to Rich's face, and panic rose in Lindsey like bile. "No, no, no!"

"Linds, chill."

She shushed Brett.

The advantage was gone as quickly as it had come. Rich clamped his legs to Moreau's waist and turned them onto their sides, getting his arm locked around Moreau's neck. Moreau's limbs were wild, lashing and kicking, fighting for purchase. They rolled and thrashed, arms and legs a gleaming blur.

"A reckless strategy. Can't see this ending well for Estrada," commented the first announcer.

"What? What?"

"Don't be too sure," the other announcer said. "He's not letting up."

The grappling raged on, and Lindsey couldn't tell who was in control. Rich, she thought. He had a leg clamped over Moreau's and an arm pinned, but Moreau had the other flailing, knocking Rich with an odd, awkward thump to the jaw.

The screen shifted to a different angle, mat-level, and Lindsey winced at the agony contorting Rich's face—agony and unmistakable desperation. For ages it felt as though nothing was happening, the two men locked in a slick knot of jerking muscle. Then at long last, Moreau reached his hand out and smacked the mat. The horn blast was swallowed in the crowd's roar and the announcer shouting, "And there you have it! Rich Estrada is the winner by submission."

"If that doesn't get Fight of the Night, I don't know what will," claimed his colleague.

Jenna dropped her pillow in time to scream with Lindsey.

"Quite the match," quipped the first announcer. "Though you can bet Estrada was hoping for a knockout."

"A bittersweet victory," said the other announcer.

"What?" Lindsey froze, not seeing any bitter side to this. "Why?"

Unlike his bested opponent, Rich hadn't stood. His trainer and some other staff member rushed into the ring and crouched over him.

"What's going on?" Jenna asked.

"I don't know. Something happened just before they went down, but…" She fell silent and sat. With help, Rich had gotten to his feet. His *foot,* rather. He held the other one a couple inches above the mat.

"We're waiting for confirmation," the announcer revealed, "but it's looking like…yes—"

"Looks like what?" Lindsey demanded, throwing popcorn at the screen. A medical official knelt by Rich, messing with his foot.

"Yes, looks like Estrada's right foot is probably broken."

"Oh, no," Jenna said, while Lindsey opted for a fouler expression.

They showed a close-up replay of the moment Rich's kick slammed the top of his foot square into Moreau's elbow, the impact looking a hundred times worse in slow motion. She swore again, earning a glare from Brett.

"Calm down, Linds. He won."

"Do you have any idea how long it takes a foot to heal? It could take a guy out of commission for *months*—"

"This time last year you didn't even know what MMA was—now you're a groupie. Give it a rest."

A guy with a mike made his way to Rich. "Your second consecutive win since you signed, and your first title. How do you feel?"

"I feel like I just broke my frigging foot."

"Unusual to see you dominate on the mat."

"Desperate times," Rich said, annoyance seeming to give

way to exhaustion. One thing was certain—he was *not* happy. Someone presented him with a flashy gold belt, but he did little more than clutch it to his ribs.

"Anything else before we let you get that foot taken care of?"

Rich said what he did at the end of every match. "Thank you, *Mamá*. Thank you, Diana." Then he added something he never had before. "See you soon."

Lindsey shivered.

The guy with the mike moved on to Moreau as Rich hopped down from the cage with the help of his corner, belt slung over his shoulder.

Jenna shook off her alarm. "Rich is healthy. He'll be back in no time, I bet." She stood and replaced the throw pillow.

"You heading out? The main event's next." *Don't leave me with Brett.*

"I think I've hit my threshold for stress. Plus I've got a client first thing, and who knows how late Mercer will keep me up rehashing this."

There was more to Jenna's hurried exit, though, and Lindsey couldn't blame her. She and Brett weren't exactly bringing out the best in each other lately. She went to fetch Jenna's purse.

"Well," Jenna said when they met at the door. "At least there's one rather selfish upside to this."

"What?"

"We'll probably get to see a lot more of Rich around the office again."

"You think?" Lindsey glanced back at the screen, a queasy sensation tumbling around in her stomach. The camera followed Rich as he was led hopping from the arena, supported by his trainer and a medic. His face was pained, glistening with sweat. He didn't look like a man who'd just won his first title fight. He looked…*uncertain*.

"I'm sure he'll come home during his rehab," Jenna said. "Mercer said he's really close to his family."

"Right. Yes." The coverage had shifted to the next match, leaving Lindsey dangling, feeling too many conflicting things: dread and relief, fear and triumph. Pride. Worry. More emotions than she'd felt in the past month combined. The result of Rich's injury? Partly. And the thought of him coming home.

"Well," she managed to say, "that's something."

Something that had guilt rising in her middle for all the times before the breakup when Brett had been making the effort to be sweet, rubbing her feet, maybe, and boom! Rich's hands. No, Brett's hands—Brett, not Rich. But he'd flashed across her mind, unbidden.

Worst of all, Brett's kisses had paled for her. She'd kissed Rich for all of three minutes—and a champagne-clouded three minutes at that—full of abandon and bad-idea excitement. Surely she was blowing the experience out of proportion. And yet…Brett had stirred nothing in her by the end, as much as she'd willed her body to respond, and indeed to keep a certain troublesome man out of her mind during intimate moments.

She bade Jenna good-night and shut the door, staring blankly at the pattern in the wood.

Rich is coming home.

And I am so royally screwed.

HE FUMBLED WITH his crutches and keys and managed to get the heavy glass door open. It was just past five-thirty. The sky was still dark, the city not yet awake.

This wasn't how Rich had envisioned returning to his home turf, post title-fight victory—limping in at dawn before the gym even opened, dropped off by his little sister on her way to an early shift at the teaching hospital. But the alternative sucked.

The alternative was to take the frigging *bus.* Show up during regular hours and get heralded as the hometown hero, clapped on the back like some prodigal son. Bad enough the board in front of his mother's church asked parishioners to pray for his swift recovery.

He was a champion now—and he wasn't supposed to be. He should have been Nick Moreau's warm-up bout, a sure-bet title-retention match to keep Moreau's streak going until the big event in Rio, just after Thanksgiving, where rumor had it a past champ wanted a comeback against him. Now Rich was the light heavyweight champ, such a shock that the promotions outfits were falling all over themselves to get busy making the merchandise no one had expected they'd need. The day after his win they'd taken him to a studio and stripped him to his gloves and belt, propped a crown on his head and photographed him for the cover of his organization's monthly magazine. There'd be a big thing on the website, too. Prince of Thieves, the headline would read. They'd interviewed him for a couple hours, all about how he'd stolen Moreau's title from under him.

Overnight he'd gone from sidebar mentions to the front cover. One desperate headlock and he was a somebody. A champion, no matter how green.

Yet Rich didn't feel like anyone worth cheering. Undefeated record aside, he felt like a failure. What good was a pit bull once its teeth got knocked out?

Back aching, armpits tender, shoulder joints raw, he swung his way down the hall and hopped one laborious step at a time to the basement, unlocking the gym's double doors.

Smelled just as it always had, he thought, flipping on one set of lights. Same as when he'd first stomped down these stairs at age twelve. You could keep your grandma's muffins—nothing said *nostalgia* to Rich like the smell of sweat and leather.

Home.

The thought had guilt squirming in his gut.

He hadn't been back since March, and a few more improvements had been made. Fresh mats, a few pieces of new equipment in the weights and cardio corner. Maybe he'd helped buy those, earning Wilinski's a much-needed boost in dues. It should have cheered him, but nothing could, not in this mood.

"The members are out of their minds," Mercer had told him. "You'd think Anderson Silva was coming to train them."

"Yeah, right. Tell them they're off by about six billion wins and nearly as many dollars."

"You'll see. Everybody's going frigging bat-shit."

Sure. Great.

Bully for them, getting shouted at by a bona fide MMA rising star. But Rich knew the truth. He'd been neutered, the best momentum of his life wrecked by a misstep, a moment quicker than an eyeblink, quick as Moreau's elbow colliding with Rich's first metatarsal. Now he was stuck limping around on crutches for the four to six weeks he'd been ordered to stay off his foot, when the last thing he wanted to feel was idle. The last thing he wanted was *time,* time to heal and to think while his muscles turned soft from disuse.

Time to worry that this funk he couldn't seem to shake might be depression. His father's bleak, hateful legacy finally come calling.

He was a trainer again. His job for the past decade, but never his passion. He'd done it for the paycheck and the free membership, for a set of keys that let him seek refuge in this underground sweat-hole in the middle of the night, those times when anger or sadness kept sleep at bay. Now he'd be one of those lazy-ass trainers, shouting orders from the sidelines. And once his bone was healed? Another couple months struggling to get back into the best shape of his life.

Stay off your feet, he'd been told and told and told.

"Shit."

Maybe this was comeuppance, karma biting him in the ass for turning his back on Wilinski's, no matter that he'd never meant the exit to be permanent. The gym hadn't changed aside from those few modest improvements, but it felt worlds different. There were the rings where he used to stalk and pounce, the treadmill he wouldn't be running on anytime soon.

He could pound on the bags at least. Those might be the key to his sanity, these next few months. His arms worked, and he couldn't remember the last time he'd had this much angst to vent.

Still, he thought, *you paid for the surgery. You did more than your old man ever—*

"Hey."

Rich turned to find Mercer crossing the threshold. "Well, well. You're in early."

Mercer flipped on the rest of the lights. "Same to you. Didn't expect to see your ugly face this soon."

"You're one to talk."

Unwilling to let Mercer come to him, Rich met him halfway, arms aching. Mercer's hug felt as it should have—nothing about it softened by sympathy. It was a relief Rich hadn't expected to register, not this deeply. He'd never been great at feeling close to guys, but this man was surely the nearest thing Rich had to a brother.

"Look at you," Mercer said, grinning with obvious pride. "Frigging undefeated pro. How about that?"

"Anybody wants to steal this crown off my head, they gotta do worse than break my foot." He cast his gaze around the space. "Looking good down here."

"It's getting there. Give it a few months and the Rich Estrada Memorial Women's Locker Room'll be up and running."

He had to smile at that. "Memorial? I'm crippled, not dead."

"You're not crippled, either. By the time we start welcoming women, you'll be back to your old self."

"Yeah. We'll see." Four months to get back into fighting shape…sounded like a life sentence with this depression dogging him, making it so hard to see the bright side of anything.

"I got plans for you," Mercer announced. He was doing his best to act as though Rich's homecoming was no walk of shame, but there was strain behind the blasé attitude.

"What plans are those?"

"Keep you off your feet."

He shook his head. "If I hear that one more frigging time—"

"Keep you off your feet and work on that broken-down game of Twister you call grappling," Mercer interjected.

Rich mustered a grudging smile. "Not the worst idea." If he was careful with his foot, maybe that wasn't such a bad use of his time off.

"Got a new jujitsu trainer lined up," Mercer said. "Nearly a done deal."

"'Bout time. He's guaranteed to be better than either of us."

"She," Mercer corrected.

Rich raised a brow. "Oh-ho. You tell her she's stuck changing in the lounge until the spring?"

"I'm sure she's dealt with worse on the road."

"Who?"

"Penny Healy."

Rich laughed. "No. *Way.*" He'd met Penny—or Steph, as she preferred to be called outside the ring. She was a kick-ass fighter, and a Massachusetts native. They'd hit it off when they'd both had matches in Vancouver. She'd told him she was looking to retire and get into training full-time. He'd given her Mercer's number, never imagining anything would come of it.

"That girl can do better. How'd you talk her into joining the Basement of Misfit Toys?"

"She wanted to move back to Mass. And I think she likes the challenge of coming on board during the whole coed transition."

"Lucky us. I'll be delighted to roll around with her."

Mercer gave him a look.

"Training-wise. Though I'll remind you some of us still have a pulse, even if Jenna's made a decent man of you. You gonna take her last name, by the way?" he teased. "Monty'd be dancing in his grave to know you wound up a Wilinski in the end."

Mercer checked his phone's clock. "Lemme show you the new computer system before the early birds show up."

Rich trailed him to the office. It looked less dreary than it had when he'd last been here, and their ancient software for tracking dues and schedules had been upgraded to something vastly better.

"You've been busy."

"Thanks to a boost in membership. Thanks to you."

"And Delante. Watched his fight in Reno. That kid's a frigging force."

"I think we've lost him forever to L.A."

"He was too big for this place."

"So were you."

A fresh stab of shame caught Rich in the gut. "Then what am I doing back here?"

"Gracing us with your majesty's presence," Mercer offered, then smiled. "Hope you can cope without a nutritionist and masseuse and whatever space-age equipment they got out west."

Rich cast the gym a long look through the office door. "Nah. This'll do."

"Bread and water," Mercer said, echoing their late mentor. "Anything more and you'll start mistaking the prison for a spa."

"And then what incentive is there to escape?" Rich finished. He sighed, some darkness lifting, making room for grim resignation. "Fine. Let's get my goddamn sentence started."

THE DAY DIDN'T start off too badly. Routines hadn't changed much, and Rich had never been a morning person. In the old days when he had to open, he'd shouted a lot and sipped his coffee until his muscles woke up around ten or eleven. This felt much the same, only on crutches, plus with every goddamn member who came through the door clapping his arm and wanting to rehash the title match.

He slapped a grin on his face and took it like a man.

By lunchtime, he was restless. He hid in the office under the pretense of finding his feet with the new system, but really he was fed up with everybody. At one-thirty he sneaked out in search of food, hopping up the steps to the ground floor. Twenty-two steps. Funny how he'd never counted before. And funny how he'd never appreciated how many that was.

In the foyer, his angst shifted. From frustration to uncertainty in a ragged heartbeat as he swung himself toward the exit. He slowed as he reached the glass windows that fronted the Spark offices—Jenna's territory. Lindsey's, too. He'd known he'd be seeing her, but… He was feeling too much already, without piling that old tangle of emotions on top of it.

The blinds were open and he glanced in.

Oh, shit. There she was. In profile, facing away, talking to Jenna.

She was just as he'd remembered. And what a kick in the

nuts it was, the way simply seeing her affected him. A glimpse of her smooth blond hair, her pink cheeks. That smirk, even directed at Jenna as it was now, did crap to his brain. What he'd give to see her gazing up at him in bed, wearing that smile.

Rich was used to women looking at him. Tall and built as he was, he had a polarizing effect on the fairer sex, and their stares nearly always said one of two things. It was either, *Sweet Jesus, take me now* or *You are ridiculous.* The funny thing was, Lindsey's eyes said both those things at once. Skepticism and lust all jumbled together, as if she wanted him, but wished she didn't.

And he understood why she wouldn't want to. That reason's name was Brett, he'd heard in passing.

Maybe a few drinks had had her ready to ignore such a technicality that night in the cab, but Rich wasn't nineteen anymore. He'd found some semblance of honor, somehow, from someplace. All was fair in love and war, but only between single parties. It burned him to think he'd come close to being nothing more than a slip of her better judgment.

Part of him wanted to march in there and sit right down on the edge of her desk.

You owe me a drink.

That's what he wanted to say, but that couldn't come before *So, you still with somebody?* And indelicate though Rich was, he couldn't bring himself to ask. Couldn't even bring himself to wait for the eye contact, not from those blue ones that drilled inside his skull and sucked all his vulnerabilities out through his mouth. And he had way too many vulnerabilities just now.

He locked his gaze at the exit and headed for the street, as fast as his crutches could carry him.

4

Dear God, what a week. And it was only *Wednesday*.

Lindsey glanced at her laptop's clock. Okay, technically it'd be Thursday in an hour. Which made it even worse that she was still hiding at work this late.

The preceding weekend hadn't been much better. Rich's televised injury had kicked it off on Friday, then she'd spent Saturday and Sunday avoiding Brett, searching fruitlessly for affordable places for August and fielding a lot of frantic calls from her parents.

Her little sister had gone missing, and no question it was a teenage rebellion disappearance, not an abduction. Wouldn't be the first time. At seventeen, Maya was shaping up to be the wild child Lindsey's parents had dodged with their first eight kids. She'd tried to reach Maya herself, but none of her calls had been returned. That worried her—usually if anybody could calm the girl down, it was Lindsey. Boring, dependable, middle child Lindsey. But she wouldn't be much good if she couldn't even reach her sister.

Then yesterday...

For days she'd been queasy, knowing she'd likely see Rich this week, for the first time in months. Only, when she did see him, she got nothing more than a glance at his back as he swung past the windows on his crutches, not taking the time to so much as wave. And today she hadn't spotted him at all.

Not that she cared.

Except she so completely *did*. She sighed at her own ridiculousness and went back to trolling the apartment listings.

"Knock knock."

Lindsey started, jerking upright so fast her chair rolled backward. But her panic morphed to shock in an instant to find the man she'd seen only on TV and YouTube since the spring suddenly framed in her office door. She grabbed the edge of the desk and wheeled herself back into place, managing a flustered smile.

"Sorry. Didn't mean to sneak up on you."

She rubbed at her heart. "Rich. Hi."

He returned her smile with a deeper one. One that turned all that shock into something different, something all warm and gooey and foolish. His hair was wet from a shower, flashing the memory of everything that had happened between them after that match.

"Hey, you remember me," he said.

"Of course I do." Jeez, had he forgotten they'd even made out? Or had he been drunker than she'd realized? *She* certainly hadn't forgotten about it, not the forceful sweep of his tongue or the heat of his hand on her neck. Her body blushed equally from arousal and embarrassment.

"Long time no see," he said, looking around the office. Goddamn, those dark eyes. "Late night?"

"Yeah. Um, have a seat, if you want."

Rich wheeled over the guest chair and straddled it backward. He set his crutches aside and crossed his forearms along the seat back, just as he'd done fifty times before, back when he'd stopped by to annoy her and Jenna the previous fall.

"I heard you'd be returning to us. Welcome home."

He shrugged.

"How's your foot?" She offered a sympathy frown.

"Fractured."

"I know. Oh, crap—I didn't even say congratulations. Well done, Mr. Champion. How long till you can accept that rematch Moreau's gunning for?"

"Realistically? Six months or more. A couple while my bone heals, then a bunch more to undo all the atrophying the injury's going to saddle me with."

"Must be nice to have some downtime, though."

"Yeah," Rich said, nodding. His agreement was transparently hollow. *Nice* clearly wasn't the word. See also *aggravating.* Maybe *stressful.* Or, knowing Rich, a string of cusswords, most of them starting with an *F.* "I guess. I'm not great at sitting still."

Lindsey's phone pinged. She checked the screen and declined Brett's call. They could resume their argument in person. He'd hit below the belt that morning, low enough to keep her out this late, praying he'd be asleep by the time she got home. He'd pretty much implied it was her fault things were so uncomfortable now, since she'd done the official dumping. Easy for him to judge—he could afford to pick up and move, but Lindsey couldn't swing their rent by herself. She'd been tempted to ask Jenna if she could crash upstairs in her and Mercer's guest room. But the line between best friend and boss was wide and fuzzy, plus Jenna had hired her as a so-called expert in the field of healthy relationships.... Jesus, she felt like a fraud some days.

Another ping, and Lindsey set her phone to vibrate and shoved it into her bag.

"Don't let me keep you from your work."

She shook her head. "Not work. If my clients start thinking they can call me at eleven at night, I've got some serious boundary-setting issues. And even if it was business hours, they can wait a few minutes while I hail the conquering hero."

"What *are* you doing here so late?"

"Just catching up on some admin." *You know, avoiding my life.* "You?"

"I swapped for a closing shift so I could meet with a physical therapist this morning."

"Will you have to do that a lot?"

"No, thank God. Clean break. All my ligaments and tendons and shit are fine."

"I really am sorry. I was like, screaming, all excited you'd won. I had no idea anything was wrong until the announcer explained."

"You enjoy that? My little Kerri Strug moment?"

She smiled at the parallel, comparing this huge man to that tiny gymnast from however-many Olympics ago. Though as infamous broken feet went, there was a handier reference to make.

"More like Jens Pulver. And he only won by decision."

He blinked at her. "You become some kind of MMA expert since I last saw you?"

"I guess you could say I've gotten educated." *Gotten quite good at cyberstalking you, that is.* "Not enough that I followed what happened when your foot broke, but I'm literate. And it's more interesting now that I've watched enough and heard some of the guys talk about their fights and where they're from.... More *personal.*" The grudges between fighters were as intense as infatuations, the way some interviews made it sound. Both had that consumptive, physical desire like a growling hunger, only with fighters that desire was to hurt another person, not bed them.

"Your big fight was great, broken foot aside. I watched with Jenna and my...my sort of ex-boyfriend. No," she corrected, needing to draw the line herself once and for all. "My *actually* ex-boyfriend."

One of his shapely eyebrows rose. "You don't sound too sure about it."

"Our relationship's been like a cockroach. We kept stomping on it but it just kept twitching back to life."

"That's very poetic. Remind me never to hire you to oversee my love life."

She had to smile at that. "It's over now, for sure. But we live together, so…"

"I can guess why you're 'working late,' then. Bummer. That's why I don't do relationships. Not worth the trouble."

She touched the mug on her desk, spinning it idly to distract herself from how disappointed his words made her. "That's an awfully lonely philosophy."

"Nah, I got family. Family comes first. And there is no second."

"How very simplistic." She sighed, suddenly feeling rather depressed by this heart-to-heart. "I guess that's why I'm the matchmaker, and you're the prizefighter."

"Plus, no offense—I'd rather be single than sharing a cockroach with somebody."

She laughed. "I don't know why I had you pegged for some Don Juan romantic type."

"Wishful thinking."

Indeed. She threw a pad of Post-it notes, hitting his shoulder. And just like that, they were back to how they'd been the previous fall. Dammit. Why'd it have to feel so good?

"Sorry. Guess you're not in the mood for my particular brand of charm."

She shrugged. "Everything's just such a mess right now. I'm not in the mood for anything except finding an affordable place, ASAP, so I can get the heck off Planet Awkward."

"Ah."

"I was going to stick it out, since there's practically nothing until September first, but I can't take it. I've spent the past three hours scouring the web."

"Any luck?"

"A few nice places, but too expensive. And a few I can afford but that either look like shitholes or are practically in New Hampshire. I may have to bite the bullet and shell out for a real estate agent."

"I know of a place. My mom's got a neighbor who's been trying to sublet her unit. She moved in with her fiancé and can't keep paying rent on an apartment she doesn't live in."

"Oh. Where?"

"Lynn. Two-bedroom place, top floor of a three-family house, not far from the train. Okay neighborhood. I dunno what the rent is, but more reasonable than Boston proper, I guarantee you that. Good landlord. Save you the finder's fee."

"Lynn, huh?"

He smiled drily. "It's not as bad as people make out. We just let that rumor perpetuate to keep wusses from moving in."

"Well, I'm intrigued."

"Didn't even get to the best part of all," he said with a smile.

"And what's that?"

"You'd be right on top of me."

"You're staying with your mom?"

He nodded.

Dear God, sleeping one floor up from Rich Estrada… She already spent her workdays hyperaware of the fact that he was prowling just a few feet beneath her. That might be too close for comfort. "Lynn's kind of a haul."

"Half hour on public transportation? Beats the frigging Green Line on a Sox game day."

"I dunno."

He shrugged, dropping his sales pitch. "I'll get my neighbor's number for you, just in case you decide you want the details."

"Sure. Can't hurt." She squeezed her eyes shut, trying to squish some of her headache away.

"You look beat."

"I am beat. And now I have to go home and tiptoe around so I don't wake up my ex, who's sleeping on the couch...." She gave her head a sharp shake.

"You know what you need? An outlet."

"Like what? Yoga?"

"No. You need to hit something."

"That sounds exhausting."

"No, really. Best therapy there is."

She smiled, skeptical. "Yeah, right."

"You want to try for real? Right now?"

"Try what?"

He nodded at the floor. "Come downstairs, take your anger out on something. A bag, that is. Not me. Don't need my pretty face busted up on top of the foot."

"There goes all the appeal of the invitation."

"Is that a yes?"

"I have to catch the subway."

Rich glanced at the clock between the windows. "That gives us nearly an hour. Plenty of time."

She pursed her lips. "I don't have any workout clothes."

"No need. We'll find you some gloves and I'll teach you how to throw a punch."

Why was she resisting, really? Another hour away from Brett, and it might work off some of this stress. Plus, Rich seemed to have lost all sexual interest in her since October, so that complication was moot.

"Fine."

She locked the office behind them and followed Rich down to the gym. He dug for his keys, then flipped on the far row of lights. Lindsey had poked her head down here only a handful of times, usually trying to find Jenna. It felt far bigger at night, stark and quiet. Smelled the same, though. Like sweat and rubber and...men.

Rich led her to a wall with a row of body-size leather punching bags. He turned and took her wrists, stopping her heart.

"Jesus, you got tiny hands. I'll find you some kids' gloves."

He let her go, but her jitters lingered. Rich headed for an equipment closet and came back with a small pair and a roll of cotton hand-wrapping tape. He leaned his crutches against the wall and hopped to stand in front of her, balancing on one leg.

"You right-handed?"

"Left."

"O-oh, southpaw." He took the hand in question in his large one, shooting hot, curious electricity up her arm.

"Could skip the tape, but let's make you feel authentic." He slipped the loop at the end of the roll over her thumb. "Pay attention—you're doing the other hand yourself."

She watched, fascinated. He wrapped the tape around her wrist, her palm, between two fingers, back around the palm. She stole glances at his face and downcast eyes as he worked, feeling scared and awed, as if she were in the presence of a different species. Maybe a jaguar, all sleek and dangerous and beautiful.

If only he'd maul me.

He reached the end of the wrap and secured its Velcro end at her wrist. "That's it."

She flexed her hand. "Wow. I feel badass."

"You look badass. Now do your other hand."

She fumbled her way through the task, Rich wrapping both his hands before she finished the one. She pulled on the fingerless gloves, feeling better already. Tough and capable.

"You ever hit anything before?"

"I took cardio kickboxing classes a few times, but all we did was punch the air."

"Here." He whacked a leather bag. "That's you." He hopped to the side and Lindsey took his place. "You're a leftie, so right foot in front and we'll work on your cross. Keep your legs bent, left fist protecting your ear, right fist near your chin… good. Extend your left arm…." She did, and Rich urged her closer to the bag. "Okay, guard back up. Lemme see what you got. Hit it with your left."

Nervous, she took a breath and gave the bag a lame punch.

"Don't straighten that arm too much."

She tried again, and Rich gave her a gentle tap on her ear with his padded knuckles. "Keep that guard up."

She snapped her fist back in place. She tried a few more punches, but surely her hand was taking more of a beating than the leather.

"Okay, watch me a sec. Pretend I got two working feet. When you throw the punch, use your whole body. Drive that back hip into it. That's where the power comes from, not your hand. Your fist is the grille of the truck, but your hip is the engine, giving you all the momentum. Grille won't do any damage if the truck's not moving." He demonstrated as best he could, balancing only the barest weight on his cast. Even with that handicap, his punch met the bag hard enough to rattle the chains suspending it from the ceiling.

"See that?" He threw a couple more, then to Lindsey's mingled worry and delight, he stripped his shirt right over his back. "Watch my hip."

Oh, how she watched. His hand and arm and waist and leg all worked as one, twisting so the impact uncoiled like a whip.

"Okay, I think I see." Saw more than just the technique— saw every intricate shape twitching along Rich's side and down his arm, plus that evil, evil muscle that crested from above his hip and dove down the front of his track pants. What the heck was that thing called? Should be called the *Sexalus maximus*, if it wasn't already.

"I need to twist into it more."

"Exactly." Rich hopped aside and Lindsey took his place.

She threw her next punch in slow-mo, but the difference was obvious.

"Better. Let your heel come up."

She tried a few more, and they began to land with nice loud thwacks. "Ooh, this is fun." *Thwack, thwack.* Rich poked her ear again. *"Ow, jeez."* She kept her fist up between punches.

"Try a jab now. Switch your feet—good. That's called orthodox stance."

"Oh! I actually knew that."

"Keep punching with your left."

He adjusted her form until she was landing the punches with that delicious *thwack* once more.

"Very nice."

"You think?" *Thwack.*

"Hell, yeah. You better be first in line once Wilinski's officially welcomes women."

"Let's not go nuts." She tried a combination, a jab then a cross with her right hand. *Thwack-thump.*

"Don't forget that hip. So…"

"Yes?" *Thwack-thump.*

"This on-again, off-again cockroach-boyfriend…"

Between punches, she raised an eyebrow in Rich's direction.

"Is this the guy you were seeing that night you and me…" He trailed off, letting a pointed look fill in the blanks.

She dropped her fists. "The night of the tournament?"

"Yeah."

"We were broken up, but yeah. We were together for over five years. That was one of our many off-again periods."

He frowned.

She wiped the sweat along her temple with her wrist. "What?"

"Nothing. Just being nosy."

"No, what? We weren't together that night. If that's what you're asking."

"Jenna said you guys were. She texted me in the cab."

Lindsey replayed those moments, the ones that had left her so confused and deflated—Rich's face as he'd read the screen, the immediate cooling of their activities. Her stomach twisted. It hadn't been *his* other woman that ruined things. It had been her boyfriend. Her *ex*-boyfriend. And he'd spent the past ten months thinking she was a cheater?

Crappity shit-crap.

"If I kept Jenna informed of every time Brett and I broke up, she'd fire me as a matchmaker."

Finally, Rich smiled.

"So never fear, I didn't try to cheat on anyone with you, if that's why you're being all cagey."

"Nah."

She shot him a look, unconvinced.

"Maybe a little."

Cute. And incredibly troublesome. Like a bolt, her infatuation was back, with all those doubts put to rest.

Rich straightened, turning back into his usual cocky self. "Just don't like the idea of being anybody's rebound. Tucked way down there on the supporting card."

She smirked. "Bet you think you're main event romantic material, don't you?"

"Oh, I know I am."

"You better watch that ego. If it gets any bigger you'll go up a weight class."

Inside though, this was no joke. They'd spoken enough in the past minute for their mutual interest to be embarrassingly plain. It scared her, as much as it had excited her ten months ago. Her life was a wreck. She knew better than to get involved with someone, whether that meant putting her heart on the line or merely sharing her body for a night. And with Rich, she didn't have the first clue which was at stake. Needing a distraction, she turned back to the bag, finding her rhythm with the jabs and crosses.

"Well, anyhow," she huffed. "I'm not looking for a rebound or anything, so…"

She sensed his nod in her periphery. "Understood."

"Plus you're above that role, apparently."

"Hey, I didn't say that. Said I didn't like the idea. Never said I was *above* it. I get beat up for money. What kind of standards you think I got, exactly?"

She got the bag with a sharp jab, then turned to Rich. "Charming."

He grinned, and she wanted to smack him nearly as badly as she wanted to kiss him. Her blood was coursing too swiftly, her body agitated from the conversation and the exertion. It was infuriating, wanting someone this much, being this close, but knowing how doomed an idea it was. After a few more punches, she tugged the gloves from her hands and passed them to Rich.

"Thanks for the lesson, but I need to catch the train."

"That help clear some of your angst away?"

"I think so." Though sexual frustration had taken its place, filling the void to brimming. All this time, that's what had wrecked their flirting? That he thought she was a lousy girl-friend?

"What?" Rich asked.

"What, what?"

"Why'd you look so sour?"

She sighed. "So that's what you thought this whole time? That I was awful enough to cheat on my boyfriend with you?"

"I dunno. Or maybe you were drunk. Don't get mad—we

barely know each other. I got no right to judge you. Hell, I got no right to judge anybody with some of the shit I used to get up to. I just knew what Jenna told me, and I didn't want to be that guy."

"Well, *I'm* not that girl."

"I know that now."

For a long time they stared at each other, until Rich broke the basement's eerie silence.

"I thought about you. While I was away."

A chill cooled her sweat. "Thought about me how?"

"I didn't want to, but the way things got interrupted…" He licked his lips, the gesture seeming more flustered than seductive. His gaze had dropped to her mouth, but he snapped it back to her eyes. "I dunno. I just thought about you. About what we started in the back of that cab."

Fool that it was, her heart soared in her chest. All this time she'd worried he'd completely forgotten about her, gone cold on her as quickly as they'd heated up. *I thought about you.*

"I thought about you, too."

Again, those dark eyes zeroed in on her mouth. "How about that."

She pursed her lips, so utterly unsure what she wanted. Her body knew. She wanted Rich, wanted him so badly it hurt. But if they kissed—or more—and she awoke hung up on him all over again… He didn't do relationships, and he'd told her as much not even an hour earlier. Lindsey didn't want one herself just now, but she'd lost sleep over Rich, over a *kiss,* and developed an unhealthy obsession with the man. It was already out of control. Best-case scenario, they came to a mutually enjoyable arrangement until he left again, once his foot healed. Worst case? His itch got scratched and Lindsey wound up with a broken heart the next time he went frosty on her.

"I better go." She pried her gaze off his and tore the Velcro from her wrist, unwinding the tape. He felt so…so close.

She suspected she was the kind of girl who could handle a casual arrangement. In theory, but not with this man. Anyone but Rich Estrada. Her attraction was too strong, her heart too banged up to survive the fallout.

He hopped to grab his crutches. "I'm taking a cab if you want to split it."

"No, thanks. I...I don't trust us in the back of a taxi."

"I'll walk you to the subway, then."

"No, really." Shy, she finally made eye contact, finding him smiling. It reminded her to breathe.

"I'm quick on these things," he offered, waving a crutch.

She shook her head. "My life's such a mess right now. Sorry."

"I'll be a gentleman." That grin said his words weren't to be trusted.

"No." She tossed the wadded cotton tape onto the mat. "Thank you for all this, but I have to go." She grabbed her bag and headed for the stairs, and over her shoulder added, "I'll see you around."

By the time she was striding through the foyer, her heart was pounding. She felt as if she'd just fled a mugging. Such a stupid impulse, yet when the door locked at her back with a snap and she gulped that cool night air...she'd escaped. Barely.

She aimed herself toward Park Street, speed-walking so she wouldn't miss the final train.

She realized then why Rich frightened her. Because he stirred things in her that Brett never had, not even when they'd been freshly, happily, madly in love. Rich wasn't even her friend. She didn't really know him, couldn't say she trusted him, certainly couldn't predict how he might be after they messed around.

But she knew if his reaction was to ignore her or lose interest...it would hurt more than she wanted to admit. And how could he *not* lose interest? She was just some woman who worked in the same building as he did. Rich had surely spent the better half of the past year drinking champagne with hard-bodied ring girls and fight groupies. Lindsey hated herself for even having these insecurities at twenty-seven, but come on—if Rich was a jaguar, she was a tabby. Convenient. That was her selling point, surely.

I thought about you.

Maybe. Just maybe he had. But she'd wasted too much time herself on thoughts of what had nearly been, hung up on a man who belonged to the whole damn world.

As she boarded a Green train, she thought, just once she wanted to feel like the shiny one. The one in the center of the photo, the scene-stealer. She wanted someone as shameless and sexy and electric as Rich to look into her eyes and make her feel as if she was the only person in the room. She wanted that look, and she wanted that body. She wanted the greedy, nasty sex his smile had promised her.

But sleeping with someone extraordinary was no substitute for *feeling like* someone extraordinary. And she couldn't handle being cast aside by a man like that. Not at this point in her life.

She got off the T at Brigham Circle, dragging herself the two blocks to Brett's and her building and up to the third floor. Light glowed under their door, and her heart sank. She was too wound up to play well-adjusted friends tonight. Plus it probably looked really bad, her coming home so late, hair wild from her little workout. She smoothed it as she walked down the hall.

The second she opened the door, Brett was striding toward her, still dressed in his work clothes. "Where the heck have you been?"

"At work late. Then I wound up hanging out with—"

He interrupted, saving her the trouble of having to explain. "I've called and texted, like, fifty times!" He shut the door behind her.

"Sorry. My phone's been on silent." *And I've been avoiding you.* "Is something wrong?"

He nodded, brows drawn together, but he lowered his voice. "Yeah, something's wrong." He took her arm and led her toward the bedroom. As he pushed the door, light from the hall spilled in to reveal the shape of a body under their covers, a long tangle of curly brown hair flopped across the pillow.

Lindsey felt rattled deep down to her bones. Was this some revenge thing? She hadn't come home on time, so Brett had conjured a rebound to spite her? That was just *psycho.*

"What the hell, Brett?"

The lump moved—rolling over, sitting up. Lindsey's heart dropped to her feet. "Oh, crap."

"Hi, Linds." Her little sister smiled blearily. "Surprise!"

5

FOR HER FIRST time ever at Spark, Lindsey called in sick.

Called in frantic, at any rate, waking Jenna just after seven but getting the thumbs-up to stay home. Luckily Thursdays were typically quiet, and the Boston Spark branch wasn't busy preparing for any special events that weekend. Still, it drove home that they were growing big enough that they'd need to hire an additional matchmaker or two in the coming months. A good problem to have.

She sprang into action early, well before Maya would wake—the girl was as animated as a corpse before ten. Today Lindsey was thankful for it, and thankful when Brett left early for work. She could use a few hours to get her head wrapped around this latest development. Maya turning up had made one thing painfully obvious—this routine with her and Brett sticking it out until the situation was more ideal wasn't going to cut it, not with this fresh load of chaos heaped on top of the existing pile. Enough with the waiting. Time for action.

And she had a lead on a place. Exactly one viable lead, and the only thing keeping her from pursuing it was her own stubbornness. That, plus it meant calling Rich.

"Suck it up, Tuttle."

At nine she rang Jenna's office number.

"Spark, Boston, Jenna Wilinski speaking."

"Hey, it's me."

Jenna's tone went instantly sympathetic. "How's it going?"

"It's…God, who knows," she said with a laugh. "My sister's still conked, so it's quiet, at least. Could you do me a favor?"

"Anything."

"I need Rich's number. Rich from downstairs."

"Oh?" *Tick, tick, tick.* Jenna's matchmaking gears were already clicking away.

"He told me about an apartment that's free."

"Ah. I don't think I have his number, but I'll have Mercer text it to you. You know you can always crash in our spare room if—"

"Um, no. Me, by myself? *Maybe.* But I'm not foisting a teenage girl on you guys." She'd talk sense into Maya this weekend and get her on a bus back to western Mass by Monday.

"Right. Well, I hope you find someplace. And swing by if you have the chance. I'd love to meet your sister."

"That's what you think," Lindsey said drily. "But we'll see. Thanks. Any idea if Rich is working this morning?"

"I doubt it. Mercer was down there at six, opening."

"I'll catch him when I catch him, I guess."

"Good luck."

Lindsey had just gotten the coffeemaker working on a second pot when Mercer's text chimed. She saved Rich's number to her contacts, stomach gurgling as she did so. Why did everything involving that man have to seem so irrationally… *substantial?*

After a bracing caffeine infusion, she mustered her courage. Even just hitting Call got the butterflies swirling. Damn crush, making her stupid when she had absolutely zero space in her life for it. She held her breath, heart in her throat.

Perhaps unsurprisingly, given how late they'd been at the gym, his deep voice was scratchy with sleep. "Whoozis?"

"It's Lindsey. Mercer gave me your number."

"Oh, hey." A hiss of breath, a grunt as he hauled himself upright perhaps. "Everything okay?"

"Do you think you could put me in touch with your neighbor or her landlord about that apartment? I'm desperate."

"God forbid I deny a desperate woman," he said, suddenly sounding alert. "Gimme a few and I'll get her info from my mom."

She released her breath. "Awesome. Thank you."

"Why the sudden hurry?"

"There's been a…development. Anyway. I'll talk to you later."

"I'm sure you will. Later, neighbor." With those ominous words, he hung up.

Great. Now she might have Rich Estrada underneath her at work *and* at home, in addition to that set of persistent fantasies. She drained her cup and did the only thing she could think of while she waited for Maya to wake. She began sorting her possessions from Brett's.

RICH WASN'T DUE in the gym until the early afternoon, but after Lindsey's call he couldn't drop back to sleep. He found his mom in the kitchen in her robe and slippers, leaning so close to her old laptop her glasses were practically touching the screen.

"Mamá." He leaned over her shoulder to kiss her cheek and take in that sweet rosewater smell, then dragged her chair back a few inches. "Don't sit so close—you'll burn your eyeballs out. We can't afford to keep replacing your body parts."

"Or that floor, if you keep scraping it up," she shot back, but pulled him down by the sleeve and pecked his cheek. "You going to town?"

"In a while." Ditching one crutch, he grabbed her mug and refreshed it from the pot, added that horrible vanilla creamer she loved and set it by her elbow. "I need Maria's number, if you have it."

Slow as a glacier, she slid the cursor across the screen to open an email. "Maria from upstairs? Why?"

"A woman who works in the office above Wilinski's is looking for a place."

"What kind of woman?"

He smiled at the question as he poured himself a cup and took a seat at the table. "A professional woman. Late twenties. She's a matchmaker for that company Mercer's fiancée owns."

Her eyes widened. "Oh. Maybe this woman, she can find you a good wife."

"Don't hold your breath, *Mamá*."

"A nice woman to come home to between all these fights, all these cities. So you won't get distracted. By temptation."

He smiled wanly. Lindsey was maddeningly tempting on her own. "What kind of *novela* do you think I live in? I got enough women to worry about between you and Diana."

"Your sister is a good girl," his mother intoned. She wasn't wearing her cross at the moment but she pressed her fingertips to the spot where it would usually hang. "Up at four-thirty she was, off to the hospital."

"I know, I know. She's a saint. So you have Maria's number or what?"

She got heavily to her feet, shuffling to the drawer where she kept her address book. Her recovery had gone smoothly, but the past couple of years' surgeries had aged her a decade and stolen her old energy.

Rich swiveled her computer to see what the email was about. Follow-up appointment with a specialist. His stomach soured. He'd banked plenty of savings these past ten months, but without insurance, the bills stacked up fast and thick. Their cushion wouldn't last forever. His body went cold as he wondered what might happen once his foot healed. If he'd ever get his momentum back as a name to watch. Or if his manager would drop him like a lame horse the second he lost his so-called fluke title.

"Here it is." His mom turned with her open address book in hand. She passed it to him, and Rich put the woman's name and number in a text to Lindsey. As he hit Send, he frowned. A wasted chance to call her. Oh, well. She was probably busy at work. And he could swing by her office when he was in later, ask her in person if she'd gotten in touch. Hell, ask her over lunch, if she'd finally say yes to grabbing a sandwich with him.

It was beyond clear that his head wasn't going to get screwed on straight until he and Lindsey finished what they'd started in the back of that taxi. She could plead chaos for a while, but eventually he'd win her over. Then maybe, once they scratched this persistent, mutual itch, he could put her out of his mind as anything more than the cute girl upstairs.

Upstairs, he thought with a smile. At work and maybe here, too. She'd be hard-pressed to avoid him, then. He'd be the one who'd have to do the avoiding, anyhow—avoid letting her stare inside his brain the way she had after his Boston win, turning him into some soul-bearing, sentimental blabbermouth.

He stood and drained his mug. "I may as well head in. Grab a workout before my sessions start."

"You take it easy, Richard. You baby that foot."

Yeah, the way my father babied himself through twenty years' worth of crippling depression and wound up with a pistol in his mouth.

"Idle hands," he countered, knowing that one would resonate with her. "And these idle hands are all I got to work with for the next two months. And all they wanna do is punch stuff."

He hopped behind her chair and leaned in, putting her in the gentlest headlock, ignored her whapping hands and planted a noisy smooch on her temple. "I'll see you tonight."

As always, when he let her go she fussed with her perm, pretending to be annoyed. "You home for dinner?"

"Nah, I'm not done till seven, and I'll probably stick around for the grappling session." He didn't have a dedicated jujitsu coach hounding him here as he had in California, and all the skills he'd picked up would go to shit in a blink if he let them. Plus whatever kept his body busy. Whatever kept the darker thoughts at bay.

"You pick up butter on your way home, okay?" she called as he went to grab his gym bag from the laundry room. He shoved a clean shirt and shorts inside and slung it around his chest, checked his wallet for his T pass and swung himself back through the kitchen.

"Butter. Got it. Save me leftovers."

"Love you, Richard. You be good."

"Love you, too, *Mamá*."

Hopping down the front steps to the street, he eyed with longing the car he wasn't allowed to drive until late September. He made his way to the bus stop, leaving one set of obligations behind and en route to the next.

By eleven, Maya was up, and Lindsey's day was suddenly moving in fast-forward. She'd reached that Maria woman and been invited to meet her at one to see the apartment. The rent was at the upper end of what she could afford, but considering she'd budgeted for a one-bedroom and this place had two, it sounded like a great deal. She could always get a roommate.

Maya flounced into the kitchen, wet curls swinging, and plopped into a chair. "What's for breakfast?"

"I need you dressed and ready to go in fifteen minutes."

Her blue eyes narrowed. "I'm *not* going home."

Not today, Lindsey thought. She'd save that fight for the weekend, once she got Maya on her side, let her feel like an adult for a day or two. Surely that's what she was craving if she'd run away from their parents' house. Again. "Not home. I need to look at an apartment and you'll have to come with me."

"Good—it's way awkward around here. What happened to Brett, anyway? He used to be fun."

"Being a lawyer happened to him. Now get dressed. I'll pack you a bagel for the train."

"O-oh, the train." She bobbed her eyebrows as she stood. "And apartment hunting. Cool."

Yes, how very grown-up. No wonder Lindsey felt about eighty this morning.

They took the subway to North Station and a commuter train to Lynn, following her phone's directions.

"I like your neighborhood better," Maya said, taking in the small city.

Sure, Lynn wasn't glamorous, but after a three-block walk, the Estradas' street proved quiet and clean, and the house looked well-maintained. A three-story family setup, connected to an identical one, with sagging decks on each floor but a fresh coat of sage-green paint.

She recognized Rich's beat-up old BMW parked along the curb, but that didn't mean he was home. *Please, please, please don't let him be home.* She had to avoid him until everything calmed down. However long that might take.

Maria was waiting on the front porch, and by the time they climbed the stairs to the third story, Maya was huffing and puffing. "Oh, my...God...too many...stairs."

"You are so out of shape," Lindsey teased. To be seventeen again, eating junk food and sleeping till noon and never breaking a sweat, yet still being thin as a rake.

"Don't give me…body image…issues."

Maria or the landlord had left the place in great shape, the walls freshly painted in neutral tones. The kitchen was super-dated, with matching avocado everything, but the apartment was sunny with big rooms. The walk to the train had been barely ten minutes, the bus even closer, and Rich had vouched for the landlord.

And this place was at the top of Lindsey's list of exactly *one* affordable, available apartment.

"I'll take it."

"Yeah, you will," Maya said, clearly wowed by the concept of having an entire apartment to oneself.

Maria was thrilled, as well. She'd clear it with the landlord, and once Lindsey forked over the security deposit and August rent, the place was hers.

Crazy. And if for some reason it didn't work out, she had to stay only through November, when the existing lease was up. She beamed a thank-you to Rich, wondering if he was at work or somewhere beneath her feet.

They said goodbye to Maria out front and headed back to the station.

"Now all you have to do is, like, pack everything and move," Maya said.

"How handy that I have my little sister here to help," she said, shooting Maya a look to say she was dead serious.

Maya stared at the ground as they walked, uncharacteristically pensive for a block.

Lindsey nudged her. "What?"

"How long are you actually going to let me stay with you?"

"I don't know. I have to talk to Mom and Dad."

"Mom and Dad suck right now."

"Everyone thinks that when they're in high school."

"No, like, they *really* suck. Like, the way they sucked two years ago."

Lindsey's heart dropped. Her parents had been through a rough patch a couple of winters back—gone as far as separating for a few weeks. But they'd ended up in counseling and eventually renewed their vows. Lindsey thought they'd seemed tense the last time she'd been home, but she hadn't guessed it might be serious.

"Are you sure you're not just being dramatic?"

Immune to her own irony, Maya sighed grandly and rolled her eyes. "I'm *so* sure. I have to live with them. The *only* one who does."

Lindsey tried to imagine how things would be if she let Maya stay for the rest of the summer. The girl was almost eighteen. She wasn't a baby, and she could handle herself on public transportation while Lindsey was at work. Drama aside, she wasn't a trouble-magnet—no major partying Lindsey had ever gotten wind of, nothing with boys that sent up any red flags. Maybe a month's taste of freedom was exactly what the girl could use to make going back to face her senior year bearable.

"I'll talk to them. But you can stay with me for as long as they're okay with it."

Maya's blue eyes widened. "Oh, my God, you are the *coolest*. Seriously?"

"Until the school year starts. You may as well get a feel for independence before you go off to college. I don't want my baby sister turning into some girl gone wild, after all."

Maya shoved her fists into the air and hooted, "Spring break!" She'd always thought frat guys and sorority girls were ridiculous. "There's no way I'm going to college, anyhow. Why even waste nine months suffering though senior year when I can get a GED in like, a few hours? It's a blow-off year anyway. Everyone says so."

They reached the station and climbed the stairs to the platform, and Lindsey realized she might just have some leverage on her hands.

"I'm going to make you a deal," she said as they waited for the next train to Boston. "Provided Mom and Dad agree."

"A deal? What deal?"

"You can stay with me for the rest of the summer, *if* you promise to go back and finish your senior year."

Every trace of excitement left Maya's freckled face, annoyance dropping over her like a storm cloud. "No *way*. You just said I could stay, with no strings or anything!"

"I changed my mind."

Maya stamped her foot and Lindsey had to laugh.

"Oh, my God, girl—you're almost legally an adult. If you throw a tantrum with me, you're not staying at all."

"I'll run away. To someplace else."

Lindsey clasped her sister's shoulders. "Just take the offer. A whole month in Boston, rent-free. I promise you, by the time school starts you'll be so bored, you'll be begging to go back."

"Yeah, right."

"You're not going to get a better offer. At least with me, you won't have to babysit." Aside from Lindsey and Maya and their twin brothers, who were in college, all five of the other Tuttle siblings were married and had kids. Though if Maya agreed, it would be Lindsey who was stuck babysitting for the next month.

But c'mon. How bad could it be?

BY LATE THURSDAY afternoon, Lindsey had secured the apartment, as well as her parents' blessing for Maya to stay in the city through August. Her mother had sounded grudging, but Lindsey didn't think it was because she disapproved. If their folks were fighting again, Maya had probably been their smokescreen, and without her to direct their criticisms at, they'd have to take a long, hard look at themselves. Maybe this was best for everyone.

On Friday, Lindsey gave Maya a choice—stay home or come in to work with her. Unlike her parents, she wasn't giving her sister any spending money, and if Maya couldn't afford anything fun, she might as well tag along with Lindsey. Who knew—maybe Jenna would take pity and give everyone early release once their appointments were over.

Jenna took the whole bring-your-sister-to-work thing in stride.

"If you get sick of watching us return emails," she told Maya as she scoured the office for stray magazines, "feel free to watch TV in my apartment. It's just upstairs."

"Do you have a computer?"

Jenna frowned an apology. "Only the one I work on, sorry."

Maya had managed to lose her phone somewhere between Springfield and Boston, and was entering social networking withdrawal. Let this experiment in temporary adulthood begin.

The magazines kept her occupied for the start of the morning, then the chatty, antsy boredom kicked in. Jenna had a client coming shortly and told Maya, "If you're sporty at all, there's a kickboxing gym downstairs. My fiancé manages it. They're going to be opening it up to women soon. I'm sure he'd welcome female opinions about the space."

Lindsey was fairly sure he wouldn't, but Mercer would likely play along if it was Jenna's wish.

"I'm *so* not a jock," Maya said, flipping through *Cosmo* with renewed interest.

"I'd give you some odd jobs to do around here," Jenna said, "but we don't have any at the moment. Maybe you could ask Mercer." She looked over at Lindsey. "He hates filing and all that administrative stuff."

"Would he pay me?" Maya asked.

"He better."

Lindsey pondered the possibility, finding no downside to the girl making herself useful. At fifteen she'd been an ice cream scooper for exactly two days before quitting. In fact…if this month was supposed to scare her straight about the realities of living without parental support and send her running back to Mom and Dad and high school… Lindsey suddenly *loved* this idea.

"I'm sure they've got *something* she could do." But nothing so pleasant as filing—no sirree. "Then you can't complain about not having any spending money. Let's go find out."

She led her sister from the office toward the back stairs.

"Fight Academy?" Maya asked, eyeing the sign.

"You know that MMA cage-fighting stuff on TV? It's that kind of thing."

"Weird."

"Agreed." Exactly what she'd thought a year ago, though now she could think of a few different adjectives. *Thrilling. Addictive. Infatuation-making.* But no chance Maya would be falling for any of the guys downstairs. She liked skinny boys with trendy hair and skateboards. Guys built like Mercer and Rich were a taste most women didn't acquire until they were a little older, when hormones shifted their radar from *cute* to *capable.*

"Ew. It smells like…"

"Men," Lindsey offered as they hiked down the steps.

It was nearing the lunch hour, and Wilinski's noontime session was always popular. There were men working out at most of the cardio stations and punching bags.

Lindsey eyed the bag where Rich had taught her to punch. She could have kissed him that night. And more. Had that really been just yesterday? Now she had a ward and a new apartment and a lot of packing to do.

"It's so *sweaty*."

"It's a gym."

Lindsey didn't see Rich among the toiling bodies, and couldn't be sure if that was a relief or a disappointment. She walked to the open office and found Mercer behind the desk. "Hang out here a sec," she told Maya, and her sister shot her a look as if she'd been asked to sit tight in a shadowy alley full of junkies.

Lindsey knocked on the door frame, and Mercer looked up from his laptop. "Lindsey. What's up? Come in." His eyes jumped to the teenage girl loitering behind her, before narrowing with confusion. She bet Maya was looking similarly perplexed. Mercer wasn't exactly a cuddly specimen, with his banged-up nose and stern expression.

Lindsey shut the door. "That's my sister, Maya. She's staying with me for August."

"That's nice." He leaned over and pushed a wheeled chair in Lindsey's direction.

"It's…unexpected. My folks are having issues and she kind of ran away. I told her she can stay with me until school starts, if she promises to go back for her senior year."

"Ah." Mercer nodded. "I put my mom through that one. And Delante put me through it. I don't envy you."

"I'm hoping I can make it *just* miserable enough that she'll realize how good she has it in the burbs."

"Do I come into this somehow?"

"Jenna said to ask if there are any odd jobs that need doing, to keep her busy. Like filing."

He made an amenable face, thinking.

"But I have a better idea," Lindsey said.

"Oh?"

"Do you have any *horrible* jobs that need doing? Like wiping down all the sweaty equipment?"

Mercer laughed. "Okay, I see your strategy. It's the members' jobs to clean up after themselves…but there's always plenty of grunt work to do—mopping the mats, laundering everyone's nasty towels."

"Perfect. She's a girly-girl. This'll be the perfect culture shock. Plus, I'll know where she is."

"With Rich short a leg, we could use the extra help. I can't afford to pay her much, and it can't be under the table—this place has been too shady too long. But if she'll sign a safety waiver, I could probably offer her a bit over minimum wage. Maybe scrape together three or four hours' work a day?"

"Would you?"

He nodded. "Sure. If this place doesn't scare her straight, I don't know what will."

"Wow, thanks so much. I thought for sure I'd have to beg you."

He stood, stretching. "I'm all in favor of keeping kids on track. Usually that means teaching them to love this sport, but if your sister needs to learn to resent it, I can swing that way."

Lindsey stood and stepped forward to shake Mercer's hand. On impulse, she made a silly face and went ahead and hugged him. "Thanks."

"Thank my boss," he countered with a smile, meaning Jenna. "It's her payroll to fund."

"She found a good one in you," Lindsey added. It was a softer and more earnest comment than she'd normally volunteer, but gratitude had her feeling tender. "When could you put her to work?"

He checked the clock on his screen. "Midday sessions wrap at two. Send her down and either me or Rich will get her a waiver and walk her through the basics."

"I will. Thanks."

She found Maya right where she'd left her, seeming glued to the spot, wide eyes taking in the activity.

"Good news," Lindsey said, then lost her train of thought completely as Rich came through the double doors.

"They'll let me do filing or whatever?"

"Sort of." She worked hard to look casual as Rich spotted her. He crossed the floor, gym bag flopping awkwardly at his back with each swing of the crutches.

"You get lost on the way to Romanceville?" he asked, then nodded at Maya. "This the development you mentioned?"

"This is my little sister, Maya. She's staying with me until September. And Mercer's giving her random jobs around the gym for extra money. Maya, this is Rich. He works here. And he lives in my new building."

Rich balanced a crutch against the wall and they shook, Maya's tiny, pale hand swallowed in his big tanned one. Maya looked too intimidated to reply. They didn't build them like Rich in the Springfield suburbs.

"So you took the place?" he asked Lindsey.

"I did. It's really nice. I owe you one."

"Now you'll be on top of me at work *and* home." His eyebrow rose and she shot him a look to say, *Knock off the innuendo in front of the minor.* "Lucky me. When you moving in?"

"This weekend. God knows how."

"I'd offer to drive you, except…" He tapped his cast with the end of his crutch. "Need to borrow my car? It could use the workout."

"You've done enough, really." *Found me an apartment, got saddled with my sister in your workplace…kept me up nights for the past ten months.* "I'll let you get ready for your classes."

"See you later, ladies." He gave a little bow as Lindsey aimed them toward the exit.

Maya shot a parting glance over her shoulder. "He's so… muscly. Is he on steroids?"

Lindsey laughed. "No. That's just what you look like when

you spend eight hours a day in a gym." *And are possessed of too much testosterone.* "He's a professional. I got to watch him fight on pay-per-view last week." They headed up the steps.

"So is he famous?"

"Yeah. In that scene, anyhow."

"That is *weird.* And his job is to, like, punch people."

"Cast all the aspersions you want, but you wouldn't believe how much he gets paid."

"I think he was flirting with you."

"I wouldn't read too much into that. Rich would flirt with a potted plant if you gave it a girl's name."

Maya laughed. "So what do I have to do for those guys?"

"Oh, you'll see."

"If it's boring, like filing and stuff, I hope they'll let me listen to my iPod."

Lindsey grinned to herself. "Oh, I don't think you'll be bored."

6

THE NEXT FEW days were a blur. Lindsey missed whatever shock Maya was in store for when her duties were outlined. Had Lindsey been the one to break the news to her, no doubt a tantrum would've ensued, but thankfully Mercer had authority or intimidation on his side. Maya had dragged herself up from the gym just after five that first afternoon, smelling of disinfectant and picking at a blister on her thumb.

All she'd said was "I hate you," but it was delivered through such a weary, defeated huff, Lindsey had just laughed.

They spent Saturday packing, and on Sunday morning Brett kindly volunteered to drive the moving van. She gave him a hug once they'd lugged everything up to the third-floor apartment, not knowing when she might see him again, and feeling okay with that.

"Take care," he said, and she thanked him and told him the same. And then…

Freedom. She felt guilty for registering it, but the second Brett disappeared down the steps…it was as though she'd shed a heavy winter coat and could feel the breeze on her bare skin again.

She and Maya unpacked as much as they could before exhaustion and hunger had them calling it a night and ordering a pizza. She wondered if Rich might stop by, hearing them banging around upstairs, but he never did.

All too soon it was Monday. Maya went in with Lindsey, wanting to wander around downtown before her afternoon "slave labor" shift began.

Jenna was out of the office, attending a managerial seminar at the Spark headquarters in Providence. Lindsey had a meeting scheduled with a tough new client, Ben Reynolds. On paper, Ben was a cinch. Forty, cute and clean-cut, with a cool job in architecture and fun hobbies. The issue was that his request to meet a bright, goofy, down-to-earth professional woman was proving far tougher than Lindsey had anticipated.

Turned out it wasn't only men in search of trophy wives who were perfectionists. During their previous appointment it had become alarmingly clear Ben wouldn't settle for a woman unless she looked like Reese Witherspoon and possessed the worldliness of an ambassador and the wit of Tina Fey.

He'd barely settled in the guest chair when he started in. "What have you got for me this week? All the duds out of the way now. On to the winners."

Lindsey bit her lip to keep from getting defensive about her perfectly attractive and successful and utterly non-dud-like female clients. "I've got a couple I'd like to tell you about."

"Only a couple? What am I shelling out for?"

Her internal eye roll was epic. "I've been doing my best with your…specifications."

"Well, quality over quantity."

"I'm going to be honest with you, Ben…I've set you up with every childless, educated, preferably blond woman aged twenty-nine to forty-two in the city. And to be even *more* honest, they're all great. I'm not giving up on you or anything, but could you entertain the idea that these women aren't the issue?"

He crossed his legs, sighing. "I'm not going to settle for

someone who's good *enough*. And she doesn't have to be perfect, just perfect for me, you know?"

"What was wrong with Andrea? I thought she'd be a home run."

"She's just… She didn't want to get Indonesian food. She worried it was too spicy."

Lindsey had been careful from the start to set a frank tone with her clients, choosing blunt honesty over wishy-washy hand-holding. She was grateful for it now. "Come *on*—that's the worst thing you can give me about her? You can't overlook a lack of interest in spicy food for a chance at falling in love with someone?"

"She has a weak chin."

"Oh, Ben." She shook her head, letting him see how ridiculous she found him. That was half the battle in this business—convincing people to get out of their own way. "I'm seriously running out of women."

Something shifted in Ben's expression, and his lips curled into a mischievous smile.

"What?" Lindsey asked.

"How about you?"

She blinked at him. "As a date?"

"Yeah, why not?"

"Because I'm your matchmaker, Ben. I'm not a client."

"Off the clock, then. I'll quit the service."

"No. That's flattering, but no way."

"How come?" He wasn't being pushy. He was actually being rather cute, and if this had been a romantic comedy and not Lindsey's real life, she could even have been charmed. Especially if Ben were being played by Paul Rudd.

"Just no, okay?"

Rich passed by the office windows, pausing in the open door. He'd clearly been poised to interrupt, until he spotted her client. Lindsey beckoned him in. "Rich, come here a sec."

Ben swiveled his chair, seeming unnerved to find a large Hispanic man with a stitched-up temple standing above him, braced on crutches.

"Ben, this is my boyfriend, Rich." She made a face behind Ben's back, begging Rich to roll with it.

"Oh. Hello."

"Hey," Rich said.

"So that's why I won't go out with you, aside from all my other perfectly adequate reasons."

"You're Lindsey's boyfriend?" Ben asked, sounding surprised. Surprised she'd landed him, or the other way around?

"Oh, yeah," Rich said. "She's crazy about me."

"Um, yes. That I am." Lindsey frowned at Rich, unseen by Ben.

Ben looked to Lindsey. "How long have you been going out?"

She said, "Two weeks" just as Rich said, "Three months."

"It's been *official* for two weeks," Lindsey corrected. "We've been casual for a while now."

"That so?" Ben asked Rich, clearly not sold.

"Oh, yeah. She's into some real freaky bedroom shit like you wouldn't bel—" He broke off as Lindsey raked a finger across her throat. *Shut up, shut up, shut up.*

"Anyway, yeah. Me and Lindsey. Totally a thing."

"I'll see you later, honey," Lindsey said pointedly, and Rich departed with a smirk in her direction.

The rest of the workday passed in relative peace, Ben abandoning his hard sell, placated by Lindsey's promise to find him a suitable date by the end of the next week or refund his membership. She almost hoped she'd fail, just to get him off her plate. Though the challenge did hold a certain appeal.

At a quarter to six she found her sister in the gym. Maya had a mop in her hands, but she wasn't working. She was standing next to Rich, watching the evening grappling class. Lindsey wandered over.

"Hey. I'm ready to head home whenever these guys are done with you."

Rich checked the clock on the wall. "You girls hang out until seven-thirty and I can score you a lift with my sister."

Maya's face lit up. "Oh, hell, yeah. It takes me over an hour of work to even pay for the train and subway rides."

Lindsey shrugged. "Okay." She could use that time to strategize on the Ben issue.

"Get back to work," Rich told Maya. "Empty the trash cans when you're done with the floors."

After Maya left, Lindsey smacked Rich's shoulder.

He rubbed the spot. "Jeez."

"'She's into some freaky bedroom shit'? What the heck was that?"

"Too much?"

She shook her head, miming utter disbelief.

"What was I supposed to say? You blindsided me." To the group he shouted "Switch!" and the fighters broke apart before tangling once more with different partners.

"You were supposed to just nod and look all intimidating. My client thinks I'm a nut-job now."

"Did the trick, then. You're welcome."

"Yeah, thanks."

"You wanna thank me properly? Take me out for a drink? You promised me one, that night in the cab. Before Jenna wrecked our fun and glory called me away."

She pursed her lips, hoping her blush didn't show. She'd begun to doubt if he remembered them even discussing that.

What was the harm? She wouldn't—couldn't—misbehave too badly, what with her sister sleeping in the next room, and she could use a change of scenery after the long day. "Sure. Someplace close to home, though. I'm pooped."

"I'll take you to the finest townie bar your new neighborhood has to offer."

"Sold."

"My mother wants to have you girls down for Sunday dinner to say welcome to the building."

"That's nice of her."

"Bring an appetite. And if you're vegetarians, repent now—she's making tamales, and at least two kinds of animal will be giving their lives for the cause."

Lindsey laughed. "Sounds good."

"You know your taste for MMA?"

She nodded.

"I think it's hereditary. Your sister was busting with questions."

"She was probably just avoiding doing her work."

He shrugged, unconvinced. "I'm gonna get a pair of gloves on that girl, first chance I get."

"If you can get her interested in anything aside from Facebook drama and overpriced jeans, I won't stand in your way. But trust me, sweating is *not* her thing."

"We'll see."

A funny shiver went through Lindsey as their conversation lagged and she registered Rich's body—its nearness, the shape of his bare arms, the smell of him. In a couple hours she'd be sharing a drink with him, and a walk home. A good-night kiss? With her living situation squared away, she couldn't plead complication anymore. It filled her equally with nerves and excitement to wonder what might happen, and how their date—if that's what it was—might end.

"I'm going to wrap up some work. Meet you out front at seven-thirty?"

He nodded, gaze lingering on her mouth or chin. "See you then. Stay thirsty."

She got absolutely nothing done. She scrolled through the

Boston bachelorette database but didn't take anything in. Maya wandered in just before it was time to go, collapsing dramatically into Jenna's chair.

"Have fun at work?" Lindsey asked, shutting down her programs.

"This has got to be, like, illegal child labor."

"Beats flipping burgers, right?"

"If you say so."

As she locked the office, Lindsey heard Rich's unmistakable, staggered footsteps coming up the stairs, punctuated with the tap of his crutches. She smiled as he appeared, hoping she looked cool and blasé.

"Thanks for the lift."

"Sure thing." He led them toward the exit and Lindsey held the door. "My sister practically drives past here when she's doing her internship. Hey, there she is." He nodded to an old silver sedan parked along the curb.

Rich opened the passenger side, and as Lindsey did the same with the back door, he shot her a look. "Don't. Change of plans."

"Huh?"

He leaned in to address his sister. "These are the girls who just moved in upstairs, Lindsey and Maya." He turned back. "This is my sister, Diana."

Lindsey stooped to offer a wave and a smile through the windows at a pretty, round-faced young woman with curly black hair. Diana mouthed, "Hey."

"You mind giving Maya a lift home? Lindsey and I are going to grab a drink. We'll catch a cab later."

Apparently, Diana was game, as Rich hopped back and waved to tell Maya to have a seat.

Lindsey was confused, but prepared to adapt. "You have your keys, right?"

Maya rolled her eyes. "Yes, *Mom.*"

Good, let her be annoyed—whatever killed the illusion that life with Lindsey was going to be some thrill-a-minute adventure in urban living. "See you later, apparently. Thanks, Diana."

"Sure thing," she called, and Maya slammed the door.

As they pulled away, she turned to Rich. "Change of plans, huh?"

He smiled. "I've been waiting ten months for this drink. Realized I don't want to waste it in the neighborhood bar, getting interrupted by everyone I've ever met coming over to say congratulations."

"That's fair. Where to, then?"

Rich flagged a cab as it approached, the gesture effortless, as though vacant cabs tailed him like pilot fish. "Someplace where nobody even knows what MMA stands for," he said, putting the *Cheers* theme in Lindsey's head.

As they climbed into the back he asked, "You know of a place like that?"

She gave the driver the name of an upscale bar where she and Jenna had held a couple of Spark happy-hour mixers. She was suddenly glad she'd dressed nicely. Rich would look woefully out of place, but if she knew this man at all, he wouldn't give a crap what anyone thought of him.

The bar was on a side street a block from the park. Rich paid the driver and Lindsey held the door to the bar open so he could swing himself inside.

It wasn't even eight, but the dim lighting and sophisticated atmosphere made it feel like two in the morning.

"Here okay?" Rich led them to a booth for two in the front corner. A touch romantic, plus good people-watching through the window if they found they had nothing to talk about.

"Perfect."

The waitress dropped off cocktail and tapas menus, gaze lingering on Rich. Lindsey knew that look, and it had nothing to do with him breaking an unspoken dress code. That was the look of a woman who wouldn't mind taking body shots off most any part of the male landscape poorly hidden behind Rich's T-shirt. "I'll be right back for your orders."

Rich scanned the drinks list. "I have no clue what most of these are. You order for me."

"Oh?"

He closed the menu. "Surprise me."

"That sounds like a challenge."

"Go nuts. Whatever you get me, I'll drink."

Liking this game, she perused the list, weighing her two choices—embarrass the hell out of this oft-obnoxious man, or order something decent and maybe impress him. Or the third choice, order him something exceedingly strong and have her way with him. In the end, she ordered a pint of expensive imported beer and a cosmo.

"Thanks for this," she told him as the waitress left. "I hadn't realized it, but I needed a night out. Away from my sister, mean as that sounds."

"Hey, my sister was a teenager once. I can sympathize."

She opened her mouth, but suddenly there were no words. One good look at that handsome face, lit by the candle flickering in a glass cylinder at their sides, and her insides went all squishy, brain turning to goo. Never mind the stitches. Never mind the accent or the sheer brutality of Rich's job. He looked like the most gorgeous, sophisticated thing she'd ever seen.

He raised an eyebrow, amused by her scrutiny.

"Sorry. I spaced out."

"Long day?"

She nodded as the waitress appeared with their drinks.

Rich eyed his beer. "You let me off easy."

Lindsey grinned and swapped their glasses, sliding the cosmo in front of Rich.

He frowned. "Oh, come on. It's pink."

"I know," she said, faking commiseration. "I hate those things. But my beer looks fantastic, doesn't it? It's Danish."

He smiled—the sexiest, snidest, pursed-lip smile she'd ever seen—and narrowed his dark eyes.

"Payback for the freaky bedroom rumor you started with my client."

"Fine." He lifted his glass, implying a toast. Lindsey reached out, urging his pinkie coyly to the side.

"There you go. Very prim."

She could sense him suppressing a smile. "You really make a man fight for his dignity, don't you?"

"And you really like fighting, don't you?"

The grin broke through. They tapped glasses and sipped and Rich made a face. "Jesus. Are all girly drinks this strong?"

"Yup. And the sugar doesn't help. Here—we'll share." She set her glass between them and he did the same. They traded tastes of each, and it took only a few minutes and half an ounce of vodka for Lindsey's lips to loosen enough to demand, "Is this a date?"

Rich nodded.

She bit her lip.

"Here," he said, pushing the cosmo toward her. "Finish that and ask whatever it is you're dying to."

Feeling a touch giddy, she did. As she set down the empty glass she asked, "If Jenna's text hadn't wrecked everything that night…"

His brow rose.

"Would you have tried to…come upstairs with me?"

"Maybe. If you'd given me some signal I was welcome to."

"Oh." Lust wriggled in her middle at the thought of Rich Estrada's mouth on hers, his mind on whether or not he might get invited up to take things further.

"Would you have?" he asked.

She shook her head. "My ex-boyfriend was upstairs."

"Oh, right. And if he hadn't been?"

"I dunno. I've never done that. Invited anyone up for, you know. A one-night stand."

"Never?"

Why exactly did it sting to have him confirm that's what it would've been? It never *could* have been anything more, not with him leaving Boston so soon after, not with her own singlehood being so fresh and complicated. Not with the two of them playing in such vastly different leagues.

Whatever, let it sting. No need to overthink it.

"Never," she confirmed. "I was with the same guy for all those years. On and off, but mostly on. And even when we were off, I never did much more than go on the odd first date. It's hard to get psyched up to move on when you're moving on from somebody who feels like…I dunno. Like such a part of who you are."

"I can see that."

Making out with you was the closest I've come to sleeping with a man who's not Brett since I was… God, she hadn't felt a different man's hands on her body since she was eighteen. Since her first boyfriend, the one Brett had never approved of back when they'd only been friends. The only other guy she'd slept with.

It made her curious. About Rich. How his palms would feel, sliding down her sides, hips, thighs. How he'd smell, how he'd sound. What he'd say.

And who knew what he'd be into?

Panic shunted lust aside as she realized all the security she'd had with Brett was lost. Surely a man like Rich drew lovers like moths. He was only a couple years older than her, but their lives were so different. All at once Lindsey felt like a blushing virgin.

"Sorry," he said, snapping her from the thought. "Shouldn't have brought him up."

She shook her head. "No, no. It's not that. Just the vodka starting to work." *Just way ahead of myself, worrying you're into sex stuff I've never even heard of.* What a waste of a date with the most gorgeous man who'd ever deigned to flirt with her. She eyed their dwindling glasses. "I think we need another round."

"I know exactly what we need," Rich said, and snagged the waitress's attention. "We will have…" His gaze skimmed the menu. He pointed to something Lindsey wasn't meant to see, and the waitress nodded, heading for the bar.

"What did you just order?"

"A taste of unfinished business." He leaned back, a smile curling his lips, eyes narrowing.

She knew what that must mean, and smirked when the waitress returned with a bottle of champagne and set two flutes between them.

Rich spared the woman the rigmarole of opening it, motioning for her to let him. If it violated any safety policies, she ignored that fact, making Lindsey wonder if Rich appreciated the ease with which he got women to give him whatever he wanted. And just how easily Lindsey herself might be persuaded to do the same—let him strip the foil from her body and pop her cork with a deft, practiced hand.

She watched his arm flex as he unwound the wire, triceps twitching as he squeezed the cork free. Lindsey clapped as he poured, and this time an articulated toast couldn't be avoided.

She held up her glass. "To…" *To whatever happens when we leave here.* A wistful notion that—considering she lived with her sister, and he with his sister and mother—ought to have been a prayer and not a toast. Privacy was at a premium in Lynn.

"To our five glorious minutes in the back of a taxi," Rich announced.

"The ones from last fall, or ones I don't know about yet?"

He grinned and they drank. "That is a *very* good question. And I'll just let you wonder about the answer."

Lindsey laughed. "You're not a subtle man, are you?"

He shook his head, splashing more fizzing wine in their glasses. "Whether you're getting hit on or plain old *hit* by Rich Estrada, you will know it."

No wonder she was already reeling. Nerves had her itching for some warning she could offer, to cut him off at the pass—*nothing's going to happen between us in the taxi tonight.* But why wouldn't it?

She wanted that, insecurities or not. She was single, so was Rich. And they liked each other. If things went too far and they did have a one-night stand, it wouldn't be some shameful mistake. She'd get to watch him fight on TV in six months or a year, and maybe think, *That man gave me the best sex of my life.* And if he didn't? If it turned out flash and swagger and an insane body couldn't hold a candle to what a lover of five years could do to her…? Well, that would make getting over him that much easier.

For a couple of minutes, they didn't say a word. Rich was studying her, squinting with something softer than mischief. She returned the look, until it began to feel too intimate, too scary, and she turned her attention to the street.

"I think you're real pretty," Rich said, matter-of-fact.

She met his stare. "Thanks." *I think you're the most handsome man I've ever seen.*

"I meant what I said, about thinking about you while I was on the road."

"I'd have guessed the ring girls would be more than happy to keep you distracted." She realized as she said it, her stupid, glib armor was coming on, deflecting his compliments. She wished she could take it back.

"You probably didn't think about me," Rich said. "Sounds like you were pretty busy while I was away. Stomping on your cockroach."

She pursed her lips. But he'd given her another chance to return his sincerity, his flirtation, and she wouldn't waste it. "No, I thought about you. About what happened in the cab."

"Oh?"

She stared at his fingers, curled around the base of the glass's stem like a napping cat. "I...I think what happened..."

He sipped his champagne, waiting as she got the words out.

"It changed everything with my ex. I'd forgotten I could feel that much, just from a kiss. That I could feel that with another guy. I think it was the final nail—realizing I was missing out on feeling that stuff as long as I stayed with him."

Oh, God, why had she just said all that? Did that sound completely clingy and feely and psycho? She met Rich's eyes, scared of what trepidation she might find there.

His expression was hard to read, and for a few breaths he just blinked at her.

"That probably came out wrong," she murmured.

"I hope not. I liked how it came out."

Her blush was hot, sizzling in her cheeks and flushing her neck. "It sounds dumb, since all we did was kiss. But I don't know...I just hadn't felt that in so long. It made me sad that he couldn't make me feel that anymore." She paused and sank back against the seat. "Sorry. We're supposed to be on a date. I'd never advise my clients to start yammering on about their exes on a date."

He smiled. "Do I look like I know anything about dating etiquette?"

"When you're wearing a suit? Yes, you do."

"Right now I'm wearing a stinky old T-shirt, so trust me,

I don't give a shit what you're talking about, as long as I get to watch your mouth while you're saying it."

The blush again, and Lindsey bit her lip. Rich mimicked it, seeming to find her endearing when flustered.

"You're different tonight," he said. "Usually you knock everything I say aside like I'm chucking rocks at you."

"Do I?" She knew she did. Sarcasm was her defense mechanism, and men like Rich put her on guard. She didn't know how to handle him any better than she might a charging bear. "I'm a little drunk."

He smirked, noting she'd yet again blocked his flattery with a flick of her snarky gauntlet. "It's a good look for you."

But under the banter, something had shifted. This wasn't the Rich she knew from around the office. No bravado, no persona. There was no crowd for him to play to, only her. She'd met this Rich exactly once, in those quiet moments after his fight. She felt naked, knowing Rich could spot her flimsy armor so easily. There was no intimacy unless both people stripped away their defenses, and right now, looking into those dark eyes, she felt unmistakably bared. And it scared her. She didn't know if she could feel this way with a man, unless it was more than simple sexual attraction. Her gaze escaped out the window once more.

Rich filled their glasses and asked, "You think your sister's going to make it to September before we scare her back to western Mass?"

Was she relieved or disappointed that he'd shifted the conversation, closing the shutters on that connection she'd felt? She wasn't sure, but she rolled with it. They sipped the champagne until it was gone, talking about their sisters, about the future of the gym, about Lindsey's clients. Her anxiety receded as they fell into an easy rapport.

When the last of the champagne was gone, she checked her phone. No calls, but— "Jeez, it's after ten."

"Time flies."

"We should probably head home soon. I have to be up at seven."

"I have to be up at five, but you don't see me rushing to get my slippers on. Hey—I got an idea." He sounded a bit drunk. That didn't bode well for her own state, given they'd been drinking at the same rate, yet their size discrepancy was probably equal to a middle-schooler.

"What idea is that?" *That you take me home to your bed and ravage me?*

"Let's go to the gym and whale on stuff."

Close enough. She was eager to keep this high, liberated feeling going.

Knowing they might prove famous last words, she uttered them all the same.

"Sure. Why the heck not?"

7

THEY WOUND UP walking back to Chinatown—slow going with the crutches, but only ten minutes' journey. The air was fresh, the evening breeze cool and the night electric, enhanced by Lindsey's tipsiness and Rich's proximity. Simply being seen with him made her feel sexy. It was thrilling, borrowing a taste of his spotlight.

She unlocked the foyer's front door.

"Hang up here a sec," he said. "I'll make sure the coast's clear."

"Good thinking." There wasn't anything seedy about their actual plans, but they *were* decidedly strange. She didn't relish explaining to Mercer or some other trainer.

"Clear," he called, and Lindsey headed for the steps, excitement spiking.

She kicked off her flats at the base of the stairs. Rich rummaged in the equipment closet, returning with the cotton tape and gloves. Lindsey remembered how to do the wrapping— she'd practiced at home with a pair of tights, nerdily enough. She secured her gloves and got into position in front of the nearest bag.

"Teach me something tough. Like hooks or uppercuts or

those ones where you spin around and whack a guy with the back of your fist."

"Tough to uppercut a heavy bag, but those other two, sure."

He showed her how to throw a hook with her front fist then her back.

"Really *twist* your body."

"This is…going to hurt tomorrow," she huffed between shots. "In my…nonexistent abs."

"Hook's tough. Don't pull anything."

Weirdest foreplay ever. But each time a punch echoed up her arm, it set her nerves buzzing, got her blood pumping quicker, harder. This must be why make-up sex—or indeed midfight sex—was so intense. Spike desire with aggression and everything primal bubbling inside Lindsey burned that much hotter.

Whack.

Pain burst in her fingers. "Ow." She glanced at her hand, finding two skinned knuckles.

Rich stepped close. "No more left hook for you. Hang tight, I'll patch you up."

She gave the bag a few softer punches with her right hand while she waited, recalling some silly fantasies that were the inverse of this—daydreams in which she dabbed Rich's scrapes and sweaty brow. Damn fighter fetish.

He hopped back with a first-aid kit. She stripped the fingerless glove and tape and he swabbed her bleeding knuckles with a stinging antiseptic wipe, smeared them with medicinal goo, then carefully wrapped each in a bandage.

"Nice," he said. "First blood."

"Yeah, my own. Very butch."

He snapped the case shut. Leaning close, he took her other hand in his, tearing the strap open and tugging off the glove. Slow as a seduction, he unwound the tape, around her palm, between her fingers, over and under until he held her bare hand in his gloved one. Lindsey swallowed.

Softly, he said, "We're gonna be back in a cab together soon."

She nodded.

He slipped his fingers between hers, then did the same with her other hand, the gesture making the difference in their sizes all the more explicit. Her breaths came shallow and short.

"You gonna let me finish what we started last year?"

Are you going to let *him?* That distinction—him doing, her the target—didn't bother her. It excited her.

Her usual quips were gone. She answered without uttering a syllable, raising her head, cocking her jaw. Rich leaned in and took what she offered.

His lips tasted sweet. After a flurry of shallow kisses, he took things deeper, the slick, hot intrusion of his tongue knocking the sense clean out of her head.

He was the one with a broken foot, but Lindsey felt ready to topple, every muscle from her waist down turned to jelly. All at once it was October again. The cavernous gym was gone, and they were shut in an intimacy no bigger than a backseat. Rich's fingertips in her hair, thumbs on her cheeks. The lips she'd mourned all these months were exactly as she'd remembered, down to the very flavor of this kiss. The way his mouth owned hers... She'd follow him anywhere, just as long as this feeling didn't stop.

And suddenly she *was* following him.

They staggered a dozen paces to a weight bench. One moment they sat side by side, the next she was straddling the padded seat, seconds later her thigh had edged over his, their mouths never separating. The desire felt like gravity, an unstoppable force pulling their bodies together, never close enough. His palms were on her waist, the grazing touch hot and curious.

She stroked his hard shoulders and raked her nails down his arms, spurring his kiss. Bossy hands coaxed her hips. She did as they asked, fumbling onto his lap. With a palm on her butt, he hauled her against his chest, lips slipping to her throat.

She'd been imagining this contact for ages. The two of them pressed together, all her excitement reflected back in the restless twitching of male muscle.

In her fantasies, Rich always seemed to just turn up in her bedroom in low-slung sweatpants, face set with dark determination, crawling across her comforter and taking her without a word. Never had a weight bench featured, but she wasn't complaining.

His arms were strong. Her body tightened as she imagined him doing this during sex—holding her in his lap, dictating their motions with those gruff, demanding hands. He slipped one beneath the hem of her shirt, and the mismatched sensations of his gloved palm and bare fingers made her tremble.

For so long, she'd been fantasizing about the man from those videos—the fighter. But here in reality, he had so many more dimensions. Who Rich Estrada was had nothing to do with his stats or record or stills posted on the web. None of those could tell a woman how hot his body ran, and how that fever burned when they were pressed so close. No measure of his reach could quantify the power of these arms, locked at her ribs. She'd never met a man who seemed so elementally like *himself* in sexual mode. She couldn't have said she knew him, not until their bodies were communicating this way, without any words.

"Rich." She hadn't meant to say it. Her stubborn side was reluctant to sound so overwrought, so affected and worshipful, but here in his arms, in his lap, why fight it?

The mouth at her throat grew hungrier, the drag of his lips

sharpened by the soft scrape of teeth, rousing her pulse to a tight throb. One hand roamed up her back and tangled in her hair as the other tugged her closer, closer. Close enough for their centers to brush, and for the stiff press of his erection to suck the air from her lungs.

"Rich."

"Lindsey." He said it softly, huffed through the breath that heated her skin. The hand on her hip slid between them, up her side, and finally cupped her breast. His fingertips were warm, gloved palm neutral. She shivered.

Without even realizing, she'd begun moving in his lap. Tiny motions were all she could manage with her legs dangling, but even that subtle friction had heat building. She clasped his arms just to feel the hard muscle.

His mouth ravaged her throat, her jaw, then claimed her lips once more. As they kissed, their hips moved in a mutual rhythm. Lindsey felt desire flash and gather and solidify to a vital, physical force in her belly, all misgivings and hesitance gone.

Just as her lips grew tender, Rich released her. He coaxed her to stand and she obeyed on shaking legs. When he rose, the very size of him made her weak, the way he stared down from so high above her. She swallowed.

He smiled, the gesture plainly telling her he found whatever expression she wore amusing. Small wonder—she probably looked rabid, ready to devour him from his feet up.

"We aren't stopping, are we?" she asked.

His grin doubled every bit of arousal she felt—hot as his arms, his scent, the restless, hard body she'd felt against her own. "I hope not. But there's only so much we can accomplish on a weight bench." He ripped open the Velcro tab at his wrist.

Hell, if this was a one-time-only, no-strings opportunity, what did she have to lose? She slapped his hand as he went to tug off his glove.

"Leave them on."

His eyebrow rose. "You're one of those, huh?"

She stepped closer, running greedy palms down his chest and stomach, holding his hips and marveling at the hardness there.

He trailed the backs of his fingers down her arm. "I should probably shower, at least."

She met his gaze. "Dear God, no."

"Wow. You win—that's a new one. How freaky are you, exactly? Should I wear a mouth guard?"

"No…" She ran her palms up his biceps again, ravenous. "But maybe I should."

Rich laughed. "You're not the woman I thought you were."

She smiled at that, not merely from the flirtation but from being called a woman for a change, not a girl. And let him think she *was* freaky—why not? It was how she felt right now. Wild and free and sexy.

Despite her protests, Rich tore off his gloves and flung the tape after them. "You may not have any hygiene standards, but I know where those have been. C'mere."

She expected him to own her with more hungry kisses, but he surprised her by grabbing one crutch and taking her hand, leading her haltingly across the floor. Where exactly was this tryst going to go down? She hoped Mercer wouldn't be finding her panties wedged between the filing cabinets after they despoiled his office.

He didn't lead her to the office, but to a room beside it. It was a plain and tidy space, painted cinder block decorated with the odd fight poster, an old TV and DVD player on a stand across from a couple of beat-up recliners. A white projection screen hung from one wall.

"I never knew there was a lounge down here."

Rich left the lights off, letting the glow leaking in from

the gym be enough. "For studying match footage, dissecting the competition or your own form."

But Rich didn't have a show in mind, not one that featured anything beyond the two of their bodies. Fine by Lindsey. She'd happily study his form, live and in person.

He led her to the larger of the two recliners, resting his crutch against the wall.

"Here." He sat and beckoned her to join him.

For a minute or more, it was sweet, nearly tender. She settled sideways on his lap, calves dangling over the armrest. His kisses were lazy and deep, fingertips trailing up and down her bare arm before cupping her jaw, that touch that made her so reliably crazy. She wanted to press closer, find out if he was hard for her again. But these kisses were so sensual and slow, her brazenness abandoned her. She hadn't expected to discover this man. A rough, eager fighter, yes. A shameless man who moved more quickly than she was prepared for, sure. But not the one she was tasting this moment, the one kissing her deeply, whose steady breaths warmed her cheek.

He pulled back to look her in the eyes. His lids were heavy and she ached to see that gleam behind them, aimed down at her from above, in bed.

He didn't utter a word, but his hands spoke—they issued a simple order, tugging at her hips. She did as they asked, wedging one knee on either side of his thighs. It didn't look a thing like her fantasies, but her desire burned as hot as she'd known it would, just feeling him so close, filling her lungs with his scent. No cologne this time, only a faint hint of perspiration and the smell of his skin and hair, of Rich.

He tugged again at her hips, seating her tightly. A gasp fled her lungs to feel him so hard and ready, and though he didn't smile, she could sense a grin lurking behind those quirked lips. He knew what he did to her, and he liked that power.

Two could play that game.

She braced her hands on the back of the recliner, perfected her angle and began to roll her hips. That smirk was gone in an instant, his expression tensing with unmistakable surprise and arousal. He felt obscene between her legs, his cock just as big and hard as every other part of his physicality, just as dangerous. He swore softly.

Charged by this sudden reversal, she tangled her hands in his hair, holding his head. She'd never been this way with a guy. All…rampant. It made her feel like the sort of hottie she imagined Rich normally hooked up with, and in the moment, feeling the part was far better than looking the part.

"Goddamn, you feel good." No missing it—his voice had gone raw, as though she'd turned him into an animal, brought out the beast in him. It raised goose bumps along her arms.

"So do you."

For a moment he nuzzled her neck, the caress caught between desire and tenderness. Then she felt that scrape of his teeth along her jugular and the steam of an exhalation, and she knew any gentleness she'd sensed was her imagination's doing.

His whisper warmed her skin. "You have no idea how long I've wanted this."

Ten months and two days. That's how long she'd been waiting to finish what they'd started. Add another couple weeks if you counted the fact that she'd wanted him the second they'd laid eyes on each other. "I can guess."

"But I didn't exactly come prepared," he said between kisses, lips just below her ear.

Though part of her was disappointed, another was pleased to think he wasn't such a playboy that he carried condoms wherever he went. That their winding up here together was unexpected, maybe even special…circumstantially, if not romantically.

"I didn't, either." Lindsey had never bought a condom in

her life, and hadn't used one in years. The idea excited her—it smacked of the impulsive hookups of youth and all the experiences she'd forfeited, staying with the same man for so long and never exploiting their time apart.

But it wasn't to be tonight. "We can still…you know. Mess around."

He smoothed a stray lock behind her ear. "That we can." He laughed, a silent hitch of his shoulders and a squinting of his eyes.

"What?"

"You make me feel about sixteen again."

She pursed her lips. "I was thinking the same thing. Only I never messed around in boxing gyms in high school."

"Then you missed out." And with a gruff motion, he bent his knees, forcing her even tighter against his hips.

His mouth swallowed her gasp. Bossy hands begged her to move as she had been, stroking her desire against his.

She wanted more—their pants gone, so she could feel him against her, discover exactly how he measured up to her fantasies.

Soon the friction overtook him. He lost ownership of their kiss and abandoned the effort, cupping her jaw and pressing their foreheads together. Nose-to-nose, she heard every labored breath, felt those strong hands trembling. Between her thighs, his hips grew restless, making demands—*rougher, faster.*

He was so much more *physical* than any guy she'd messed around with. It set her nerves humming even as it banished her inhibitions.

She pulled away, openly enjoying the sight of him. That handsome, flushed face, parted lips. He wanted her. She'd done this to him. She reached between them, tugging at the hem of his shirt. He stripped it off smoothly, but she had no time to admire the results before he was peeling her own top over her head and arms.

She was as soft and pale as Rich was hard and tan, practically a different species. But when she saw how his gaze drank her in… *Angel food cake is soft and pale,* she thought. And Rich looked ready to consume her. A shiver curled her spine as his broad, rough hands grazed her waist. She shut her eyes, feeling her nipples stiffen from the mere promise of his touch.

"Jesus," he muttered.

She opened her eyes, finding his attention on his hands, palms whispering featherlight up and down her sides.

"You've got the softest skin I ever felt."

She thanked God for her exfoliating shower gloves. For bothering with lotion that morning, wearing a nice bra and shaving her legs. Clearly, her subconscious had seen this coming.

She studied him. She'd watched this bare torso a zillion times—on TV and online, in person down in the gym. But never like this. She stroked his chest, glad he didn't wax as some fighters did, loving the soft feel of the hair sprinkled there. It blazed a dark trail down the most gorgeous set of abs she'd ever touched, and she wanted to ease his waistband to his thighs and see exactly where it led.

She wrapped her arms around his neck and began moving. He cupped her breasts, tightening her body in a hot wave, spurring her motions.

Between rousing kisses he asked, "How far you wanna take this?"

"I don't know."

His fingers posed the question a second time, slipping low to fiddle with the closure of her pants. Her silence answered, and she let him free the clasp and lower the zipper. With a few moments' fumbling, he slid them down her thighs and she kicked them away. Before she got settled, he untied the drawstring of his warm-ups and pushed them low on his hips, erection hidden by taut gray cotton.

When he tugged her against him once more, everything felt different. Cool air and worn leather on her bare legs, and the thrilling press of his cock along the soft seam of her sex.

"Rich."

He closed his hands over her hips, urging her forward and back in tight, slow thrusts. She held his shoulders. She was already wet, the cotton of her panties dragging against him, making the friction feel as sinful as penetration.

"That okay?" he asked, still guiding her motions.

She stammered, "Y-yeah."

His hands edged higher, following the flex of her waist. "Show me how you like it."

Lindsey cast aside every lingering scrap of self-consciousness and let her body lead.

She slid her clit along the ridge of his cock until she found the perfect pressure. "Lower the chair."

He found the lever and the footrest creaked, rising as Rich eased the two of them down. She got her knees where she wanted them, seating herself higher. Now when she pulled back, she felt every inch of him. She shut her eyes and swore through a smile, overwhelmed.

Rich's patience waned. His hands were bossy, urging her movements, hips shifting between her thighs.

She smiled down at him. "Do you need to be on top?"

He cleared his throat and quit fidgeting. "I'm just wound up. I've been wanting this for so long. I'll knock it off."

"No." She tugged at his arm. "I like you wound up."

With a couple more tugs he relented, and they wrestled around so Lindsey was on her back. She held in a grin. Being in control of Rich's big, capable body was a thrill, but having him above her… She stroked his arms as he got his knees braced, and wrapped her legs around his hips.

He cupped her head, owning her with deep, bold kisses. She mourned his mouth when he leaned back, but the disappointment was brief. His thick arms locked beside her waist as his hips began to move, their rhythm echoing up the length of his extraordinary torso.

She was staring. She didn't care. Rich's body, tight with desire and undulating with this basest of labors, was the most exciting thing she'd ever seen. Watching him stirred her arousal as much as the rough stroke of his erection between her legs.

She held his shoulders, his muscles restless against her palms. "Rich."

"Tell me you thought about this."

"I did." *At times when I shouldn't have. Long after I'd decided it was a lost cause.*

"I thought about you in every crappy motel I crashed in between here and San Diego."

Simple flattery or the truth? All those nights she'd conjured him prowling across her covers on his hands and knees…had he been imagining something similar, three thousand miles away? She realized she didn't care if it was a line. She *felt* that desire burning down at her in this strange room, and that was truth enough.

His arms were warm, roped with locked muscle. His cock was just as hard, just as hot, dragging with maddening friction along her lips and clit. The glow leaking from the gym made his skin gleam, reminding her how it shone under the bright lights of an arena.

She snaked her arm between them, and when her hand closed around his erection, he stilled his hips. She rubbed him through his shorts, just to feel it—this one part of the male body that even fighting wasn't crude enough to expose. He began to move, the rhythm of his hips matching her strokes, quickening the contact.

She expected an arrogant remark from this brash man, a rough hand clamped over hers, forcing the touch and asking, *You like that, don't you?* But his only sentiments were excitement and desperation, broadcast in every ragged breath.

This is actually happening. Rich Estrada was hers, somehow. Hard in her hand and panting with need. Wanting her.

She let him go and cupped his face with both hands, shuddering as he took control of the friction. "You feel so good."

A tight laugh. "I promise the way I pictured this, I at least got us into a bed."

"Me, too."

But reality felt better. Urgent. A little twisted. And she had him just as she'd wanted—above her, in charge, pleasuring her with gruff, powerful strokes, even if those strokes drove him against her, not inside.

She rolled her hips, lengthening every motion, dragging the pleasure out, out, out. Her core gave a hungry squeeze and she imagined how good he'd feel, stripped save for the barest skin of latex, excitement buried deep, her sex slick from how badly she wanted him.

"Rich."

"Yeah. Come on." No smooth words of seduction, but so exactly what she wanted to hear in that harsh accent.

Hand on his shoulder, the other arm locked around his waist, she held on for dear life, filling her lungs with his scent, her ears with his low moans and ragged breaths. Reality blurred until the only force in the world was this pull, this hot ache boiling inside her, this man the only person who could end the wanting. Her hips sought the friction, chasing what her sex demanded. He read her cues and gave everything she asked for.

When she came, it was from that—from that sensation of

being *given* this pleasure, and from his mastery of his body. Sensation gathered in a knot, drawn tight and hot, fraying and finally coming undone, one snapping thread at a time. She hugged him tight, quaking against the cruel pressure of his cock. As she cried out, he went still, sparing her anything more than his hot weight against her swollen lips through the wet cotton.

Her chest was heaving. She registered her nails biting into his back and released him, embarrassed. "Sorry."

"Don't be."

He let her catch her breath, though she felt his desire throb against her with every beat of his heart, his sexuality a living, breathing force.

She stroked his hair. "You...now."

He started slowly, testing her. Within a minute she was desensitized and he resumed his earlier pace. In the wake of her orgasm, desire built anew, but it was his needs she wanted satisfied. And to see this capable, brazen man rendered helpless, if only for a few seconds.

She memorized the flex of his hips with her palms as her eyes took in that face, strained from something so different than combat...yet the expression so nearly identical. His lids were heavy, but every breath or two, that penetrating gaze broke through.

Who on earth are you? This man she barely knew, yet whose body felt so right. She held on, watching as he came apart.

"Oh." He pressed his cheek to hers, overcome.

With a desperate grunt, he reached between them, pushed his shorts down and freed his cock. She felt the smooth, slick skin of his crown, then heat lashed her belly as he came.

His groans faded, muscles falling slack. Suddenly it was just the two of them, in this dim, silent room, ripe with the smell of sex.

She held his arms, feeling crazed, and saw that frenzy mirrored in those dark eyes.

Rich leaned over the armrest and grabbed his jettisoned shirt, wiping Lindsey's skin.

She studied his gorgeous face while he was distracted. *His breathing's just the same when he's spent from fighting.*

Tossing the shirt aside, Rich settled on his forearms, dropping his chest and face to hers. He brushed their lower lips together, back and forth, and laughed, barely more than an exhalation.

She stroked his hair. "Well."

A proper kiss, then he leaned back, glancing around the room. "This place'll never look the same again."

A silly wave of pride accompanied his words. Why she should feel surprised, she wasn't sure. He'd told her he'd thought about her. Why shouldn't he remember them fooling around, weeks or months or maybe even years from now? Perhaps every time he set foot in this room.

With a quick, sure motion, Rich flipped them and hauled her sideways on his lap, sitting up as the recliner snapped to attention. He held her under the knees and shoulders, as though he'd just carried her across a threshold. He kissed her mouth, his vibe playful once more. The desperate version of this man was fading, locked away behind the carefree shell.

Had she lost him, just like that?

Needing a distraction, she ran her hand over the squiggly black characters tattooed down his ribs. "What does this say?"

"That's the first thing I learned to say in Thai. It translates to something like, 'Who do I get to hit next?'"

"You were there a year?"

He nodded, fingertips grazing up and down her arms. "Got my ass handed to me for the first month. Everybody wanted to fight the gigantic American *farang*. Went from being a pretty damn good boxer to getting beat shitless by teenagers who were a foot shorter than me. Most humbling experience of my life."

"Rich Estrada, humble?"

He kissed her. "Don't tell anybody."

She touched the ink on his shoulder, slipped her palm down the gulley of his back, where the largest design hid, all these eclectic passport stamps.

But the thought of him leaving again… It made her sad. It also made her feel warm and hungry and possessive. Her chances with this man were limited. Hell, they might amount to no more than this evening. It made her want him with a fierceness she'd never experienced.

His fingers dawdled, playing with her sweat-damp hair, and he kissed her throat. A happy sound hummed through her neck.

She toyed with his hair. "What?"

He met her eyes, smirking. "You thought about me, huh? This past year?"

She blushed. "Yeah. I did."

"All this time."

She nodded. She ached for him to return the confession again, cement the mutuality she'd felt earlier, believing this longing had been two-way. But all she got was a smugly cocked eyebrow and a self-satisfied smile. Rich the performer.

Or…or was that other Rich the performer? The one who'd professed ten months' infatuation? Was *this* the real him, this shameless scoundrel not a persona after all?

What had just happened had meant something to her, for better or worse. But to Rich, it was entirely possible it had been nothing more that the latest in a long string of impulsive encounters. She needed to remember what the two of them were, first and foremost—friends. Friends who happened to want desperately to wind up in bed together. A perfectly fine thing to be. No need to get hung up, wishing it could be more.

Only, she so completely *did* wish that.

"It's late," she said.

"Yeah."

He let her legs go, and once Lindsey had made it to her feet, he did the same. He cinched his drawstring as she slid her pants up her legs. Unison, good. Let this all look equal. Let him believe she felt as he surely did—checkbox ticked, curiosity satisfied. Let him think this had been simple to her, too. That she wouldn't get a stomachache, waiting to run into him again, having no clue what—if anything—she meant to him.

She knew what he meant to her. A stranger in many ways, yet this man affected her as none had before.

He pulled out his phone and opened an app. "I'll get us a cab."

She tugged on her top and smoothed her hair. "Good idea."

She'd spent the past couple years compartmentalizing emotions where she and Brett were concerned—surely she could do the same with Rich. She wasn't some sloppy romantic, not the way Jenna was. Her heart was her commodity to guard and offer, not some external entity that a man like Rich could seize when it suited him and return when he was done, tender and smudged with bruises.

He found himself a clean shirt from the locker room, and they made their way upstairs, standing side by side in the balmy August night.

Lindsey didn't know how she felt anymore. A little embarrassed, still thoroughly smitten. And sleeping in her new bed, in her new room, with Rich lying somewhere beneath her…

She wasn't going to be making sense of this tangle anytime soon. Not as long as that body was within ten miles of hers. To say nothing of ten feet.

8

RICH ROSE EARLY, not rested enough but eager to start his day—to get his mind focused and his body lost in the endless to-dos of training.

He started the coffee and woke his sister, then kissed her goodbye at the curb outside Wilinski's at five-thirty.

Time for work. Time to get his thoughts off Lindsey—her body and her smell, her soft skin under his palms, her voice in the dark of the gym.

He'd needed last night. Needed the release and simplicity of sex, and a chance to feel like a man again, after the way his injury had castrated him. A hit of the crowd's admiration shining up from those blue eyes.

Sex was great. Lindsey was great. She was special, even—too special to treat like some fuck-buddy from the office upstairs, even if that was all *he* was to her. But special or not, she didn't fit into his plans. She couldn't stay lodged in his brain like a splinter, niggling at him night and day. Maybe in some alternative universe where Rich had only himself to worry about, or an imaginary future when his sister and mother were secure and he was free to start some new family… But that wasn't the reality he lived in.

In reality, he was sidelined for months and earning a fraction of what he had been. His focus had to be singular, homed in on his recovery and nothing else.

With twenty minutes before the gym was due to open, he poked through the computer system. Scaring up members and hunting down dues had been Mercer's arena since Monty's passing, but after fifteen-plus years in this basement, Rich knew his way around the books. He pulled up the file where Mercer tracked their active membership, pleased to find it had gone up a healthy fraction since he'd last looked. He jotted new names, then slid open the filing cabinet by his foot and flipped through the applications.

Every form had a slot for referrals and goals, where new members were asked what brought them to Wilinski's and what they hoped to get out of training, be it a pro career or simply a good workout. Rich pulled the newest members' files, and laughed aloud when the very first one confirmed his egotistical suspicions.

Written in the referrals space was "Want to train where Estrada does."

Others mentioned him, too. The happy, queasy feeling in his middle didn't have much to do with arrogance, he realized. It was *pride,* to be staring at proof that he was giving back, even as an absentee. Always in the background these past ten months had been the guilt—he'd kept his mother and sister foremost on his mind, but this place was family, too. It lifted a weight to believe he'd done good, after all. He might be the most half-assed trainer the gym had ever boasted, but he was attracting new members, even if he wasn't mentoring any.

At six he propped the doors open, and the mood carried him through the morning sessions. He couldn't do much more than hop around, holding targets and shouting orders, but he did it with more energy than he usually mustered this early in the morning.

At one o'clock he spotted Maya coming down the steps

from the foyer. Mercer was holed up in the office, meeting with the web designer he'd hired to haul the gym into the twenty-first century. Rich couldn't tackle much of the tidying up on crutches, so the girl was welcome to the cash. Though she looked less than enthused to be here.

Rich swung himself toward the entrance to meet her. "Glad to see your smiling face."

"I wasn't smiling."

"And I wasn't serious. But I'm still happy to see you. I got a disgusting job to get done and you're just the woman to help me."

"Great." She wrinkled her nose. "I'll never get used to how nasty this place smells."

"Oh. Did no one tell you? It's a boxing gym."

She rolled her eyes. Ah, the charms of youth. "Not much of a gym."

"It's got showers and rings and shit to hit. That's all you need in a gym. Anything more'll make you soft." A lie, kind of. Rich had experienced some of the nicest MMA camps in the country this past year, and Wilinski's could stand a few more of their amenities. But in essence, he meant what he said. If fancy gyms made the best fighters, the UFC would be packed with nothing but rich guys who could afford to start at the top, and that simply wasn't the case.

"So what do I have to do?"

"Tuesdays are quiet, and we're overdue for a hardcore scrub-down. You're gonna help me lift these mats, one section at a time, then we're disinfecting everything. Top, bottom, floor, everything."

"That's sounds terrible."

He smiled. "Oh, it is."

Rich shifted everyone to a different section of the floor, and Maya took his orders, filling a couple buckets with diluted antiseptic solution. It wasn't glamorous, but it felt good to get on his knees and just scrub, foot forgotten. It reminded him of being a kid. His parents couldn't afford the membership, but his mom had begged her way into some deal with Monty Wilinski, so Rich got to train at a discount if he helped with this stuff on the weekends. It was humbling then, but now, not so much. This place had done so much for him, scouring this floor felt oddly like a penance.

Maya was less Zen about the task. Her face was red within a minute and she insisted the solution was giving her a rash.

"I'm counting how many times you complain," Rich said. "When I get to five, you're finishing on your own."

That shut her up.

Miserable as she was…there was something there. That willful gleam in her eye that told Rich she might hate every second of this job, but she wouldn't quit until these mats were as fresh as the day they'd been delivered. He fought for money, she cleaned for it. And though neither pursuit was pretty, both stuck at their duties for more than just a check.

The time came to turn the mats over, and Rich couldn't hazard the task one-legged—Maya was on her own. They were connected in sections, each weighing at least eighty pounds, and a flexible, slick eighty pounds at that. They twisted when she attempted to flip them, fell back on her or slipped from her hands. But she didn't bitch. She didn't quit, not even when some of the guys working out laughed, watching as the mats flopped back on her for the umpteenth time. There was hate in her eyes, but she channeled it away from a tantrum and into an ugly strain of determination. Rich wouldn't have expected he and Maya Tuttle had anything in common aside from a home state and an attitude problem, but there it was—that grudgelike persistence, that screw-you streak that came out when someone expected them to quit.

He liked this kid.

Once the mats were done and the gym smelled more

bleachy than usual, he rattled off a fresh list of tasks. "And don't drag your feet just because you're paid by the hour. I got my eye on you."

Maya set to the jobs with a mighty sigh, scuffing toward the spent water cooler jugs, literally dragging one foot. Rich shook his head with a smile.

The afternoon sessions were winding down right as Maya wrapped her final chore. Rich stopped by the equipment closet, then approached her, hand behind his back. "Good work. Got a reward for you."

She wiped her sweaty brow with a forearm. "Oh, goodie. Do I get to clean the toilets with a toothbrush?"

He tossed a pair of gloves at her chest and she caught them.

"I have to disinfect these, too?"

"Nope. You gotta put those on."

"This is a reward how?"

"Free lesson with a bona fide celebrity fighter."

Her expression was deeply unimpressed and Rich shot her a withering look. "You're still on the clock. Humor me."

She tugged the gloves on and fastened the straps, squeezing her fists open and closed. "How many other people have worn these?"

"You don't wanna know. C'mere." He led her to the heavy bags. "Your sister's no slouch, so I got some faith in you."

"I don't. I've never hit anything before." She eyed the bag, nerves seeming to overshadow the petulant brat act.

"Just give it a whack. With whichever's your dominant hand."

The limpest, saddest jab.

"Come *on,* that was pathetic. Hit it hard. Pretend it's my face."

"Oh, yeah, like my sister would ever forgive me for that."

Rich ignored the remark, as well as the hot jolt of satisfac-

tion it gave him. He'd done too well today at avoiding thoughts
of Lindsey to relapse now.

"Hit it."

This time, she did. Not an elegant punch—absolutely no
technique, but a good thump. "Not bad. Knock that stance
open, right foot in front. Keep some bounce in your legs.
Good. Now hit it again with a cross."

"A what?"

"With your left. Keep punching till I tell you."

She did. Lazily at first, though after a dozen hits and a couple directives from Rich, she got into it. The strikes landed
harder and louder, and that mean glint had returned to her
eyes.

"Let that back heel come up. Don't force it—let it come
up naturally. Better. Get that left fist up next to your face."
He adjusted her guard. "Keep that there or I'll whack you
in the ear."

"I like Mercer better," she huffed between punches.

"Now switch feet, and show me your right."

She shifted her stance and Rich circled to her other side.
He flicked her unguarded ear and she swore, dutifully raising her fist.

"Cross. Cross cross cross until I say stop."

Damn, this girl was good. Rich whistled across the gym.
"Hey, Merce."

Mercer's brows rose. He gave the departing web designer
a final handshake and wandered over. Three members tailed
him, intrigued by the novelty of a teenage girl doing anything in Wilinski's aside from waiting for her boyfriend to
finish his workout.

"Check this out," Rich said, nodding at Maya.

She shot the new witnesses to her torture a glare, but the
annoyance only seemed to sharpen her focus. *This girl would
move a mountain just to spite somebody.* Rich's kind of student.

"That's not bad," Mercer allowed. "What kind of jab's she got?"

"What's a jab?" Maya asked Rich.

"Hit it with your front fist."

She tried a few, quickly finding her power, then tossed in a cross.

"She's got a combo!" teased one of the members.

Rich flicked her ear and she swore again.

"Oh, she's clearly yours," Mercer said. "What'd you teach her first? Crosses or cusses?"

"She came standard with those. Switch your stance. Check out this left."

A couple more guys wandered over, drawn first by the oddity, but kept rapt by the undeniable fact that the girl could hit.

Maya was red in the face, winded and possibly mortified, but no way was she quitting before he let her. Stubborn as he'd been at that age. And still was.

"Okay, okay, break."

She stared Rich right in the eye and gave the bag a final, resonant whack before dropping her arms. Her eyes said what her lips didn't. *I hate you.*

"Grab some water. I wanna see if you can kick at all."

He watched a dozen R-rated retorts pass over her face before she stalked to the water cooler.

Mercer laughed. "Dude, she wants to murder you."

Rich grinned. "Ain't it beautiful?"

"Girl can hit, though. If she actually enjoys this, I'd love to break Steph in on her next week."

Rich shook his head, smile deepening. "This one's all mine."

LINDSEY LOOKED UP from her email as Jenna entered the office, surprised to find it was pushing four. Maya had said she was working downstairs for only a couple hours, but they must have found some extra tasks to keep her occupied. Fine by Lindsey. She'd tackled a ton of paperwork with the office all to herself, and staved off distracting memories of what had happened the night before, one floor down. Mostly.

"Hey, boss. How was your PR thing?"

Jenna had been out since lunchtime, a meeting for a publicity opportunity. There was something weird about her face. Her mouth was twitchy, expression stiff.

Lindsey frowned. "Are you suppressing good news or awful news?"

"I'm not— Well, fine. I am." Jenna dropped her charade and grinned. "It's good news."

"You're already engaged, so… Oh, crap, are you pregnant?"

Jenna made an exasperated noise and set down her briefcase. "It's good news for you, and for the business."

Lindsey sat straighter, intrigued. "Really? What?"

"Well…"

"Spit it out, you're killing me."

"Here." Jenna opened her case and pulled out a copy of a slick Boston arts and culture magazine. "You've read this before, right?"

"I've seen them around."

"They called a couple of weeks ago. They're doing their yearly feature on Boston's most eligible bachelorettes. They wanted to know if I could recommend any of our clients."

"Oh, that *is* cool. Who were you thinking of? Oh! What's-her-name! That woman who started the combination tattoo parlor and bakery. She's hilarious."

"Not her. But they did love my recommendation—so much so, they want her to be the woman featured on the cover as the lead story."

"Wow, excellent. So who?"

Jenna bit her lip. "You."

Lindsey blinked. Then frowned. "I'm not a client."

"No, but you're single. And you're awesome. And you're a matchmaker *and* a former wedding planner. They loved the idea of an independent, single woman, so comfortable helping others find their happily-ever-after. Plus you'd look great on a newsstand. What do you think?"

"I think…I think I don't know."

It was at once thrilling and terrifying. Lindsey wasn't desperate to settle down, but her breakup was recent enough that she wasn't exactly wearing her bachelorette status as a badge of honor.

Still, this *would* be great for business. And she was undeniably intrigued by the prospect of having a big deal made of her, if only for a day. How often did a nonbride get to feel that special?

Jenna clutched the magazine. "*Please* say you'll think about it."

"I'll definitely *think* about it. It's, um… Oh gosh, thank you for even suggesting me. It's incredibly flattering. But give me a day or two to hunt down the last issue and see if they made the women look empowered or completely tragic." She recalled a certain episode of *Sex and the City,* not eager to suffer Carrie Bradshaw's humiliating fate in a similarly spin-able situation.

"You'd be *perfect.* Like Spark's high-profile ambassador. And you do so freaking much around here, you deserve some spotlight."

Lindsey pictured all the photo shoots she'd witnessed for engagement announcements, all those fancy lamps and lenses, makeup and hair people fussing over the bride. She could enjoy that, and without the fiancé, even. Tempting.

"So this is business-relevant, right?"

Jenna nodded.

"So if tomorrow my morning is as quiet as the calendar makes out, could I spend it looking into this…proposal?"

"You may. In fact, if any unexpected client issues pop up before lunch, I'll tackle them for you."

"Okay. Sold."

Jenna did an undignified little celebration dance, spinning around on her chair.

"Calm down. I didn't say yes."

"Last year they did Boston's most eligible bachelors, so check two autumns back."

"I will."

Maya appeared in the doorway, and it took one glance at her posture and her beet-red complexion to know that something was amiss. Lindsey's mood went black.

"You okay? You're all flushed."

"Tell your stupid boyfriend I quit."

Jenna looked to Lindsey so fast her ponytail should've cracked like a whip. "Wait. Whose boyfriend?"

"Either," Maya snapped. "Her boyfriend, yours—tell any of those guys I *so* quit. I'm never going down there again."

Lindsey ignored whatever puzzled look Jenna was surely shooting her on the topic of an undisclosed boyfriend.

This was no simple tantrum. Protective older-sister mode kicked in, and Lindsey wheeled her chair over, dead serious. "Sit down. Did something happen? With one of the guys from the gym?"

Maya chewed on her answer, tears glistening in her lower lashes.

Lindsey touched her arm. "Tell me." *Tell me, and may God have mercy on whatever man said or did something to make you cry.*

She huffed out a breath, rolling her eyes. "He made me punch the stupid bag."

"Who did?"

"Rich."

Lindsey frowned, suddenly more confused than angry. "Okay... Why are you crying?"

"Because he was a *jerk* about it. And everyone was watching and he made me feel like an idiot."

Rich was grating sometimes, but Lindsey never would have described him as *cruel.* "I'll talk to him." She shot Jenna a questioning look and got a nod of approval. "I'll be back in a minute."

She stomped down the steps, her protective side melding with a zillion unresolved, uncomfortable emotions regarding her and Rich's noncourtship. He was chatting with Mercer by the bags.

"Hey." She marched over, resisting an urge to give him a sharp shove. "Why's my sister crying?"

His smile dissolved. "Crying?"

Mercer looked deeply uncomfortable and excused himself.

"You made her hit stuff while everybody watched?"

"I—"

"That girl doesn't have an athletic bone in her body, and you go and haze her about it in a gym full of guys who must seem like middle-aged men to a seventeen—"

"Whoa, whoa." Rich put a hand on her shoulder, but she shrugged it off, taking a step back. He steadied himself on his crutch. "I didn't haze anybody. And everyone was watching because she's frigging *good.*"

Lindsey frowned. "What?"

"She's good. She can hit. Listen—I was just having a little fun with her. I wasn't making fun *of* her, I swear."

"She's a teenage girl. You can't just make her do that while a bunch of older men watch. Do you have any clue how uncomfortable that would make her?"

His brows rose. "No. I guess I don't. The teenage girls where I grew up were as tough as the guys."

"Well, Maya's not one of them. And you freaked her out."

"Where is she?"

"In the office."

"Lemme apologize to her."

Lindsey crossed her arms. "I think you've done enough damage."

"C'mon. I got a sister, too. Don't take her home before I can say I'm sorry."

She considered it. "You can follow me up, but if she doesn't want to hear anything from you, you leave her alone."

"Deal."

They made their way up the steps, Lindsey not slowing for Rich's benefit.

"She really is good," he huffed between hops. "I'd train her if she'd let me."

Maya Tuttle, a kickboxer? Lindsey wanted to laugh at the very idea, but part of her was intrigued. Maya had never shown a protracted interest in any particular activity or subject, or been stand-out talented enough to be praised as special by any authority figures. Surely that was part of the reason she was ambivalent about going back to school.

"Stay here," she said when they reached the foyer. She entered the office, finding Maya on her laptop, checking Facebook. Jenna was in the private meeting room on a call, judging by the muffled, halting conversation.

"Rich would like to apologize to you," she told Maya.

"I'm not going back down there. Ever."

"He's come up. Would you like to hear him grovel, or shall I send him away?"

Curiosity passed over Maya's face, something that told Lindsey she liked the revenge inherent in this offer. She'd always been keen to guilt an apology out of her parents and siblings. "Yeah, I guess."

Lindsey went back to the hall, feeling like a principal. "Okay," she told Rich, "you get five minutes."

He followed her back inside. Lindsey loitered by the door as he took a seat on the edge of her desk.

"Hey," he said, laying his crutches on his thighs.

"Hey," Maya muttered.

"I'm sorry if I upset you. I thought you were just mad at me for bossing you around. Since I'm kinda your boss."

Her lips quivered, undermining her tough-girl act. "You guys were making fun of me. Because I suck."

He laughed, shaking his head. "You don't suck."

"Yeah, right."

"I've been boxing forever. I've seen plenty of guys come through those doors who've been punching stuff since they were toddlers, expecting to be told they're the next Frazier or Silva or Victor Ortiz."

"I don't know who any of those people are."

He smiled. "No, I bet you don't. But hardly any of those kids who show up, thinking they're something special, turn out to be much good."

"How can you tell *I'm* any good, just from that little bit of punching?"

He shrugged. "Trust me, your technique's busted. But for somebody who's never hit anything before, you've got some power. Plus that death glare you were giving me…"

Lindsey smiled. She knew that glare. Her sister could hold a grudge like no one else.

"I've seen a thousand guys come and go down there, but you got something nine hundred and ninety of them never will. My old mentor used to call that 'the magic.'"

Maya looked embarrassed, but from flattery now, not humiliation. "I probably just got lucky."

Rich eyed her shrewdly. "Gimme five one-hour sessions

with you, after your next set of shifts, and I promise I'll get Mercer to give you a raise."

She straightened. "How much of a raise? Double?"

"I'm not a magician, kid."

"I want twelve bucks an hour. At *least*. And I want to get paid for the time I spend getting taught."

Rich blew out a long breath. "You're killing me here."

"And I'm not buying any equipment."

"Fine. I'll train you on the clock. Twelve bucks an hour. Retroactive *after* I get my five sessions. And I'll pony up for your gear." He put out a hand.

"Twelve *at least,*" she reminded him, but shook nonetheless.

"Come downstairs a sec. I'll give you some DVDs to watch for homework."

Maya made a big dramatic show of reluctance, but followed him out the door.

Once they'd disappeared, Lindsey laughed aloud.

9

THE WEEK PASSED quickly. Lindsey agreed to do the bachelorette article, and was secretly getting more and more excited about it. She'd found the previous issue on the same theme, the profiles all flattering.

Maya had completed three of her so-called private lessons with Rich, and though she staggered up the gym's steps complaining of blisters and sore muscles, the second they got home she was cuing up the latest DVD she'd been lent. Lindsey only hoped her sister wouldn't fall so madly in love with fighting that it would steel her refusal to go back to school. She might need to research MMA gyms around Springfield and break it to her parents that their erstwhile couch-potato daughter might possibly be bribed into academic compliance with a membership. She could guess their reaction.

"We let your little sister stay with you, and within a week she's into *cage fighting?*"

Lindsey had her argument ready. "Beats boys or booze."

Saturday and Sunday were gobbled up by unpacking and decorating, and Diana lent Lindsey her car so she could shop for the essentials lost in her quasi-divorce from Brett. Maya was kept busy as well, only at Wilinski's. There was a two-day seminar for newbie fighters, and Rich and Mercer had invited her to participate, provided she help with the setup.

Rich might be showing an exceptional interest in her sister, but it was clear any interest he'd had in Lindsey was gone. Snuffed dead in the wake of their messing around. Lucky him, to have burned his infatuation clean away that night in the gym. It still simmered hot inside Lindsey. She wished she could go cool and casual as easily as he had.

Late on Sunday afternoon she changed out of her housecleaning clothes and into a skirt and tank. She could smell the feast awaiting her—the savory scent of Rich's mom's cooking had wended its way up two floors to make her mouth water. Maya got home as Lindsey was curling her hair.

"Hey. How was it?"

Maya leaned in the bathroom doorway and shrugged. "It was pretty cool." Never one to openly enthuse, this translated roughly to *It was freaking awesome!*

"Were you the only girl?"

"Yup," she said, the word all haughty with pride.

"What'd you learn?"

"Lots of stuff. Tons of kicking. I hit this one kid so hard, he fell over backward."

Lindsey shot her a look, alarmed.

"Don't spaz—he was holding a big pad thing. But Rich clapped for me and everything. Or maybe he was fake-clapping for the kid, for falling over. Either way."

Lindsey smiled, secretly wishing Rich would quit doing things to make her like him so damn much. If he could just go back to being an arrogant caricature, she could go back to believing her attraction was purely physical. Maybe once his foot healed, the strutting rooster would return and remind her why this crush was not a thing to be taken seriously.

"Check this out." Maya proceeded to show off a sampler of bruises and scrapes. Part of Lindsey was horrified, but she was far more proud to think maybe her sister wouldn't grow up into one of those women who fell to pieces over a chipped nail.

At seven they headed downstairs. The door to the bottom unit was open, and Rich, his mother, Diana and a handsome young black guy were standing around the kitchen. It was sweltering with the heat of summer and cooking.

"Oh, my God," Maya said, breathing in dramatically. "It smells even better down here."

Rich spotted them and whistled to cut through the chatter. "Hey, quick intros! Lindsey and Maya, this is my mom, Lorena." They all shook, then Lindsey shook Diana's hand as well, having not properly met her the night she'd given Maya a lift. "And my sister's no-good boyfriend, Andre." More handshakes. Andre's big, warm smile said he was used to this ribbing. "Now introduce yourselves to a drink. Dinner's ready in what, *Mamá?*"

"Ten or fifteen," she said, peeking under a pot lid.

Rich waved Lindsey and Maya toward the counter, set up with glasses and wine and soda.

Andre and Diana wrestled an extra leaf into the table and added a couple mismatched chairs from the next room.

Before long everyone was seated with heaping plates of tamales and beans and steamed corn on the cob. Lindsey and Maya took their cues from the others, peeling the leaves away before discovering they'd wasted their entire lives until this moment, never having tasted tamales.

Rich was different with his family. He nearly always seemed relaxed, but there was a deeper warmth to him tonight. He razzed Diana's boyfriend at every opportunity, though Andre gave nearly as good as he got. Lorena was quick to disparage the odd cussword, but even quicker to laugh. The easy company and wine and *way* too much delicious food lulled Lindsey into believing everything was simple. That she hadn't been invited to this house or this dinner by a man who both infatuated and confounded her. For an hour, life was blissfully uncomplicated.

Lorena grew tired early, and Lindsey was proud when her sister volunteered to help Diana with the dishes. Lindsey cleared their places, then settled down at the table with the guys to finish her wine. Rich looked happy, slouched way back in his chair, legs spread wide.

She no longer wondered why a man of nearly thirty would still be living at his mom's house. Their family dynamic was just…different. Culturally. If any of Lindsey's brothers moved home with their parents, they'd all wonder what had gone wrong. But the Estradas seemed tighter-knit. Plus, Rich was the man of the house, and in their family that seemed to truly count for something.

She and Maya thanked the Estradas profusely for dinner and said their good-nights. As they headed back upstairs, Maya patted her belly. "Oh, man. I hope they invite us down every Sunday."

"Hear, hear."

Their place felt empty and quiet after the energy of Lorena's kitchen. Maya promptly stole Lindsey's laptop and set herself up on the couch to watch whatever homework she'd been given—old boxing matches, documentaries, MMA specials, fight flicks spanning the gamut from classic to campy. Lindsey smiled every time her sister muttered a surprised, "Whoa!" or "Nice" in response to whatever she was watching.

Lindsey prepared for the coming week. She hand-washed the silk top she wanted to wear for her first meeting with the magazine people on Wednesday, and opened the door to the fire escape. She breathed in the heady August air. A clothesline ran between their building and the neighbors' across the wide side driveway, and she pinned her top and reeled it out, liking how old-fashioned the chore felt.

"Hey."

She screamed.

Not a loud scream, but more than a yelp. She glared, finding Rich sitting on the steps that led down to the second floor. He was facing the other way, twisted around to smile up at her. She fisted her skirt tight to her thighs.

"So modest," he teased. Like he hadn't gotten her down to her panties in the gym.

"You scared the crap out of me."

He shrugged an apology.

"What are you doing here?"

"I live here?"

Her annoyance faded with her adrenaline, and she descended a few steps to take a seat halfway between the landings. "I mean, what are you doing on the fire escape?"

"I used to smoke out here. Now it's just where I come to sit. Watch people come and go. Clear my head. You have a good time tonight?"

"Possibly *too* good a time. I can barely walk, I ate so much."

"I'll tell my mom you said that. It'll make her week."

"Your family's really cool." Lindsey loved her own family, and they were a fairly functional bunch overall. But an hour spent crammed around a table in Lorena's overheated kitchen had felt warmer and more familial than the Tuttles' traditional Thanksgivings, everything arranged just so in the rarely used dining room. "You're all so easy to be around."

"These days, yeah, I suppose so. It's been a good year."

"My little sister's camped out on the couch, watching old fight videos. She seems to have lost interest in any and all Kardashians, so I owe you."

He grinned. "She won't be ready to actually spar with anybody for a while—she's got, like, negative cardio capacity. But stuck in with all those other beginners at this weekend's clinics… She's got the instinct, if not all the skills."

"Weird. She usually hates sweating."

Rich covered his mouth, yawning widely.

"Aw, did we tire you out? When's the last time you had a day off?"

"Haven't since I got back. But any money's good money, and if I wasn't working I'd be there most of the day anyhow, training or loitering. Still, not too excited that I gotta be up at the ass-crack of dawn to catch a bus…. Man, I miss driving."

"In that death trap you call a car? Why haven't you bought a new one?"

"It does the job. And it's what I can afford."

"Even with all that prize money?"

"Prize money's gone. Spent or set aside for emergencies."

She frowned. That was a lot of money to blow through, considering how big his payday had been for the Albuquerque fight barely two weeks ago. What on earth did he do for fun on the road? "Maybe after your big return."

Rich's tone went a touch flat. "'Fraid not. It'll take a couple more high-end matches before I'll have any cash to play with."

"You have gambling debts or something?"

"Nah. My mom's got this heart condition, and no insurance company will have her for less than a fortune. She's been through a bunch of surgeries the past couple years."

Her suspicions morphed to sadness. "I'm sorry to hear that." Not wanting to make Rich continue to crane his body, she brushed past him, down to the second-floor landing. She sat as demurely as she could and stretched her legs in front of her. The slats felt funny, digging into her thighs through the light fabric of her skirt, but she liked it. It felt…urban. Like her new neighborhood. Like sitting on this fire escape with a foul-mouthed townie who bled for money.

"Plus you wouldn't believe how much I pay for my own insurance, given my job description," Rich went on. "And my sister's in her nursing program, and I gotta subsidize her until she tricks some poor sucker into marrying her."

"Some poor sucker like Andre?"

"We'll see. She moves slow with guys. But whoever the sucker, it'll be me footing the bill."

"Damn. Why do you have to take care of everybody?"

"Because my father's not here to do the job. It's just how we do it. Cultural thing, I guess."

The door beside Lindsey was open, and she leaned over to steal a peek at the barest kitchen she'd ever seen. "I'm guessing you always eat downstairs. Don't you even have a table?"

"It's just me on the middle floor, and I'm a mama's boy, so yeah."

"If my mom cooked like yours does, I wouldn't bother, either."

"Not much going on in the second floor except sleeping and showering. My mom and sister won't come up here, not since my dad passed away."

"Oh." She'd always assumed that Rich had been raised by a single mother.

"But I don't care. Nobody goes in the room where he passed anymore, but I sleep in the other bedroom. My mom can't even say 'the second floor' without crossing herself."

"What…what happened to your dad? He died young, it sounds like."

Rich stood, doing a very poor imitation of apathy as he stretched his injured leg. "He shot himself."

She shivered. "Oh."

He looked her in the eyes, deepening the chill. "And before that, he was a pitiful waste of space. If he thought his family was better off without him, he was right."

She felt herself recoiling, wanting to curl up and protect herself from his callousness. It wasn't directed at her, but it unnerved her all the same. She and Rich were friends, though their sexual attraction had been more potent than their platonic bond. They were close, but not on a level that let her know how to relate to him now. And she imagined that was the point. He'd put a wall up between them, and not by mistake.

"I'm sorry if your dad…sucked."

He huffed a silent laugh and shook his head, as though he could think of no word harsh enough to adequately disparage the man. Then he spoke, contradicting his expression slightly. "He was a gentle guy, at least. I'll give him that much." He took a seat once more, one step closer to Lindsey.

"It must be hard, having to fill all those roles."

"That was my mom's job." His tone lost a measure of its darkness. "Being both parents and the provider."

"Until she got sick?"

He nodded.

"Is that when you started fighting?"

"Nah. I started boxing when I was in middle school."

"Oh, damn."

"But it hadn't been about money before." He linked his hands, staring down at his flexing fingers. "There's no money in boxing, not at the bottom. I did it because it was the only thing that…I dunno. That made me feel anything, aside from angry. That made me forget for a few minutes that my mom prayed for my rotten soul every night, and cried herself to sleep, worrying about where I was headed."

"Ah."

"But after my dad was gone and she had her first real emergency, I was twenty-four. I was a high school dropout and I was good at exactly one thing. My old mentor, Jenna's dad, had already sent me to Thailand. That trip changed me."

"It humbled you, you said."

He met her gaze. "It did. I was surrounded by all these guys who understood fighting the way I did—as their only option. And it drove home this feeling like, *this is all you've got.* The only thing I'm good at. If I don't make something of it, I may as well take a page out of my dad's book and put a gun in my mouth."

She winced.

Rich hung his head. "Sorry. I got some dark shit in my skull."

"It's okay. We all do, from time to time." And she could sense Rich didn't vent his very often. Noxious thoughts needed airing, or they'd poison a person's perception of the world. If Rich had to talk about this, she was strong enough to hear it.

"It just became clear, if I didn't make it fighting, there was nothing else for me. No place I fit where I was respected, where I felt...I dunno."

"Worthy?"

"Maybe. Or just, like, useful..." He trailed off, clearly struck by some thought or other.

"What?"

"Nothing. Anyhow, it's not a matter of loving the sport for what it is. I *don't* love it, not the way some guys do. I *need* it. I'll never be like Mercer or our mentor, happy just teaching people."

Lindsey remembered how he'd spoken to Maya in the office, and realized she didn't entirely believe what Rich was saying. Even if he did.

"Then my mom got hospitalized and we found out how many procedures were on the horizon, and I just had to go for it. MMA was taking off and I talked my way into any paid fight I could get. Real shady ones. Ones that only paid fifty bucks, or only paid if you won. I fought three times in one week, I remember."

"Oh, God."

"It was insane. But I paid for my mom's first heart stent in cash. No installments."

"Wow."

He smiled, watching his fingers once more. "And it felt frigging *good*. I don't think she was ever proud of me before that. And I don't think she was all that proud that I paid her bills by beating people up, but it was more than my father had provided the last ten years of his life. And I wanted her to believe she could rely on somebody. So I just kept going."

"Now here you are on the main card. Light heavyweight champ."

He shook his head. "Now here I am, crippled and useless till my foot's healed."

She wanted to move, wedge her butt next to his on the stairs and touch him. To comfort him, though she sensed Rich wasn't a man who welcomed empathy. Instead, she said, "You're not useless. Not as long as you keep training, getting ready for the next opportunity."

"That's about all that's keeping me sane." He laughed, the noise making relief bloom warm in Lindsey's chest. "Damn, I've been talking your ear off."

"I don't mind. You're easily the most interesting person I know."

"Then you oughta get out more. But how about you? Anything exciting going on with your clients?"

She felt her cheeks heat. "Not with my clients…though I guess I do have something kind of interesting going on."

His brow rose.

"I got invited to do a magazine article. The cover story, about Boston's most eligible bachelorettes."

"Wow." Rich blinked, eyes glazing for a moment. "That's exciting."

"I don't think it's because I'm glamorous or anything. They just like the paradox of a matchmaker and former wedding planner being all comfortable with her singleton status or whatever. But it's great for Spark. And…"

"And?"

"And I dunno…I'll get to dress up and be photographed. After all those years I spent fussing over brides."

"Congratulations." He smiled, though the warmth didn't meet his eyes. Lindsey's pride drooped as she wondered what he really thought of her big opportunity. Maybe it didn't seem that big to him at all. What was some local magazine feature compared to millions of people watching you on live TV?

"It's getting late." She stood, finding her back sore where the rails had pressed. "And you have to be up before dawn."

He got to his feet and Lindsey handed him the crutch leaning against the rail. "Come in for a minute." He nodded to the open door.

"Um…"

"You want a glass of wine? For the first time in a year I can drink without my training team treating me like a criminal."

She hesitated, then Rich shot her a cheesy, swarthy look, cocking his eyebrow outrageously. "I'll show you my belt."

She laughed. "Okay, fine." Why not? She needed to get it in her head that she and Rich were good as friends. And she *wanted* them to be friends, if that was all they were destined for.

Then she glanced his way and saw something in those dark eyes. A warmth that was far from friendly.

Something far, far better than friendly.

Lindsey flipped on the light by the door. Taking in the kitchen, she had to laugh. There was nothing in the way of food aside from a giant tub of whey protein and a line of supplement bottles on the counter, and no furniture save for a weight bench and a rack of dumbbells.

"Fighting really is your entire life, isn't it?"

"Just about." He locked the door. "You stick my mom and

sister in Wilinski's, and you pretty much got everything I ever cared about, all in one place."

"What will you do, someday when you retire?"

"Hell if I know. Shame to waste this body." With a smirk, some of his swagger returned, his darkness left outside to blend with the approaching dusk. "Maybe I should look into exotic dancing."

She laughed.

"I'm not kidding," he said, though he clearly was. "I got rhythm." To demonstrate, he rolled his hips for her and advanced with a couple steps that, even on crutches, proved the man did indeed have some moves. "Don't be casting aspersions on my fine Colombian ass. We can salsa before we're out of diapers." He crowded her with a few more outrageous steps.

"You win, you win. I'll start carrying singles."

He went to a cabinet and flashed a bottle of wine. "Red okay?"

She eyed it, wondering if this was a terrible idea, what with the return of shameless Rich now official.

"Just a small glass."

He found a corkscrew. "I got sent gift baskets by everybody under the sun after I broke my foot. May as well share the wealth."

She joined him at the counter and accepted the glass he poured her. "To your mom's cooking. And the fact that I won't need to eat again for two weeks."

"Amen." They clinked and sipped. "Before, when I'd get a fight around Boston, I'd have to burn off at least ten pounds to make weight. Never had to do that once on the road. Now I know who to blame." Rich took another sip, looking puzzled. "Is this any good?"

"I like it. But I like any dry red."

"I'll make a note of that."

All this week, they'd been doing so well—an exemplary

imitation of a plain old friendship. A little flirty, maybe, but nothing like after the tournament or down in the gym that night. But now...

Maybe it was the wine, and the fact that every time they shared a drink, they also wound up sharing one another's mouths. Whatever the reason, Lindsey felt the atmosphere shift, a giant question mark hanging in the space between their bodies. Another floated in her head.

Can you handle it, if you hooked up again? If you woke up liking him more than ever, and he just went back to how he was, like it never happened?

She didn't know. She only knew how her body would cast its vote, and those instincts couldn't be trusted. Not around Rich, certainly not around Rich and alcohol.

He took another sip, gaze glued to hers above the rim of his glass. After swallowing he asked, "You want the tour?"

She managed a strategic joke, needing to take the temperature of the invitation. "Why do I suspect it'll be comprised mainly of your bedroom?"

"Because you've got a dirty mind."

She gave him a little glare and he offered a way-too-innocent shrug in return. "Take it and find out."

She relented. Rich waved a crutch, and she obeyed, preceding him into the hall, carrying his glass for him. They had the same floor plan and he sneaked by, sweeping them past the closed door to the living room.

"Bathroom," he said, flipping on the light. Surprisingly tidy for a man used to the daily ministrations of motel staff.

"Please don't tell me your mom cleans up after you in addition to cooking."

"My mom had her heart valve replaced last winter. What kind of a selfish jerk do you think I am?"

"Thank goodness."

He grinned. "My sister does the cleaning."

She sighed her annoyance and Rich shut off the light. "Not my fault I've been spoiled. Plus I bring home the lion's share of the money around here, and usually carry it in bleeding. I'm not gonna apologize for being a caveman."

"You better find yourself a real traditional girl to marry."

"That would certainly please my mom." His smile softened. "Though personally I'd rather find a snarky feminist to roll around in my sheets with."

She blinked, knocked senseless for a breath at how obviously he meant her. "I see."

He stood a bit straighter. "Unless you're all done with me, after last week. Personally, I thought we had some unfinished business…but maybe that was just me."

"I dunno." She wanted to say more, demand some answers. *If you're not done with me, why'd you go so cool after that night? And if we take things even further, will you go straight-up cold come morning?*

But those were demands you'd make of a boyfriend, or of a lover you thought you might be getting serious with. Rich was basically home on shore leave.

Though if she couldn't voice those concerns, perhaps she shouldn't waste time worrying about them. Not when the invitation in front of her now felt so simple. She upgraded her response to a shy "Maybe."

Rich replied without a single word. He leaned close and caught her lips in a soft, slow kiss. Nearly innocent, if not for the shallow flare of his breath giving away his intentions. He kept his eyes glued to hers as he straightened, taking all his heat away.

Lindsey swallowed. The wine in the glasses she held trembled.

"You probably expect guys to be all suave, huh?" he asked. "You must coach them on that stuff, as a matchmaker."

"Thankfully, no."

"But that probably wasn't real smooth, my just asking flat-out if you wanted to mess around."

"I know what you do for a living, Rich. I never expected subtlety to be your strong suit."

"Oh, good. I like a gal with low expectations." And with that, he freed a hand and put it to the small of her back, nudging her toward the open door at the end of the hall—the bedroom directly below her own. Good Lord, she really *had* been on top of him this entire time.

She set their glasses on a bookcase and found the light switch.

"Oh, *no*." She laughed, taking in the five full-length mirrors screwed flush along one wall, facing the bed. "Tacky much?"

He rolled his eyes, passing her on his crutches. "This has been my room since I was a kid. I used to shadowbox in here." He turned, smirking, then leaned in to plant a kiss on her forehead. "Why you gotta make my innocent childhood sanctuary into some kinky sex den?"

"You have to admit, it looks bad."

"To a pervert, maybe." Another kiss, on her temple this time. "How many chicks you think I sneak in here? My mom and sister are downstairs."

She looped her arms around his waist. "Like that would stop a man on a mission."

"Maybe not. But admitting to a woman I still live with my mother usually does the job."

He kissed her softly, again and again, coaxing her back a step at a time, crutches brushing her arms. A strange seduction, but somehow apt. She felt the mattress at the backs of her knees and sat. Rich set his crutches aside and joined her, tugging at her arm until she kicked off her shoes and lay down with him.

I'm on Rich Estrada's bed. When they were simply hanging out, she forgot for long stretches that he was famous-ish. Wouldn't those stupid Courtesan groupies just *hate* her if they could see? She shoved the petty, pleasing thought aside as he cupped her jaw and kissed her lips.

Far more exciting than messing around with a minor celebrity was messing around with Rich. On Rich's bed. A queen-size bed, a soft black cotton comforter. Nothing flashy, just the place where this extraordinary man slept, in this room where he'd grown up. Surely the most mundane space in his world, yet Lindsey felt positively giddy. This big mattress after the confines of the weight bench and recliner...like a playground. And she wanted to climb Rich like a jungle gym, tumble all over with him, wrestling and laughing and being ridiculous.

She stroked his chest through his T-shirt, and his hand slid over her shoulder, down her arm, then found her waist. Misgiving flared. They'd gone much further together, but tonight felt different. Her previous recklessness had been replaced by something cautious. Plus this was not a flattering angle for her belly, considering how many tamales she'd stuffed it with. Rich slipped his hand beneath her shirt, multiplying the horror.

"I love how soft you are," he murmured.

She bit back a sheepish smile, anxiety melting. "And here I was, lamenting however many pounds I gained at dinner."

"You feel perfect to me." He kissed her neck, and any last scraps of worry she felt fled with her deepening breaths.

His lips and tongue teased her throat, the contact growing hungrier as her body gave him approving cues with heavy exhalations, her palms admiring his shoulders and arms.

She combed his hair with her fingers. "You're such a gym rat. I worried...I dunno. I just worried."

"Got no time for scrawny girls. I like a woman I can roll

around with, without being scared of breaking her. Sometimes I look at you, and I just want to *squeeze* you. You look so soft."

She laughed. "I'll take it."

He pulled back, locking her eyes with his, black as pitch in the low light. "Lemme undress you."

She nodded. "Okay."

He went about it slowly, regarding each inch of skin as though he'd never seen it before. And when he unclasped her bra, he did indeed reach new territory. His gaze roamed her, then his hands, warm and strong, and finally he lowered himself to his elbows, cupped her and brought his mouth to her nipple. Her flesh pulled tight, and a sigh fled her throat, fingers fisting his hair as she struggled to process the sensation, at first too much, but soon—perfection.

Swinging his leg over her, he straddled her thighs, kissing his way down her belly. As he dawdled at her hips, his fingertips dipped inside the band of her skirt, dragging back and forth, back and forth, the light contact making her crazy. He tugged the stretchy fabric down to her knees, lips taunting her thighs, then her mound as he took in her scent through the cotton of her panties. She let him strip her completely naked, insecurities burned away by the heat in his eyes.

She curled a finger. "Come here."

He edged up the bed and helped her with his shirt, then the complicated process of getting his pants off over the cast.

She'd watched him fight, dressed practically just as he was now, only these snug black shorts didn't conform to an athletic protector. The cotton did nothing to hide his excitement, and she found her palm sliding down his chest and ribs and hip, edging closer.

He took her hand, leading it where he wanted. She roused equally from his bossiness as from the feel of his cock, thick and stiff against her palm. As he kissed her, she found a rhythm, stroking him in time with the hungry sweeps of his tongue, his flaring breaths. Between them, he took her wrist and eased her hand inside his underwear.

"Oh." His voice excited her as much as the hot drag of his bare skin against her palm.

For long minutes she pleasured him, loving his sounds and the restless fidgeting of his body, the heat and power of him wrapped in her fist. When he found the control, he returned the caresses, his overheated clumsiness far hotter than some masterful touch. Their kissing dissolved, coordination lost to need.

Against her lips he asked, "This is going to happen, isn't it?"

"It better."

With a grin, he ditched his shorts and moved his knees to the outsides of her hips, leaning over to open a dresser drawer. He set a condom beside them on the bed, then popped the cap on a bottle of lube. "Would you…?"

She took it and squeezed a small measure into her palm. The slick liquid was cool, Rich's cock all the hotter in comparison. He sucked a harsh breath through his nose as she swept her fist down his length, moaned softly as she stroked it back up. She watched his abdomen tighten with every gasp and moan. Watched his expression, lips parted, lids heavy as his eyes recorded the motions of her hand. She spoiled him with slow, luxurious pulls, and soon enough he joined the action, pumping his hips, driving his cock in and out of her slippery grip. The sexiest thing she'd ever seen.

"It made me crazy," he murmured. "That night in the gym, when you touched me. I wanted to push your hand inside my shorts so bad. And feel your bare skin on mine."

"So did I."

"But you didn't."

She swallowed. "You make me…shy."

He smiled faintly. "Do I? I kinda hoped I made you wild."

"You do that, too. You do a lot of confusing things to me."
She tightened her fist to give him a taste of the incapacitation
he made her feel with the merest heated glance.

Rich shut his eyes and slowed his movements, seeming
to reach a limit. She stilled her hand as he caught his breath.

"You ready?" he asked.

"Yeah." She let him go.

He opened the condom and rolled it down his erection in a
slow, sensual stroke. That, on top of the novelty of the act…
Lindsey felt a kink working a new groove into her sexuality, imprinting her with a trigger that only watching a man
sheath himself could spring.

She marveled at his weight as he knelt between her legs—
the biggest man she'd ever been with, in every way. The sight
of him angling his cock to her lips deepened her excitement.
Her body was so primed for this, he slid inside with a single,
slow push. The intrusion drew a moan from her chest, but
the sound was pure pleasure. She grasped his shoulders. Rich
was silent for the first handful of thrusts, gaze locked where
her body joined his. Then his eyes met hers and a low groan
warmed the air between them.

His voice was tight. "Christ, you feel good."

"So do you."

He shut his eyes, seeming to savor the experience as he
eased inside with slow, measured motions.

A million words flashed through her brain, aching to be
said. *You have no idea how many times I've imagined this.
About us, and this exact moment. And the reality of it puts
all my best fantasies to shame.*

But it was Rich who next spoke.

"I like it pretty fast, usually."

Not quite the poetry she'd been composing herself, but it
made her smile nonetheless. "That's fine by me."

When he found his pace, she joined the motions, spurring

him with her hips, welcoming every push, sharpening the angle each time he withdrew. His arm muscles locked, actions growing rough. So perfect. So exactly how this man ought to be in bed. Just as he'd been in her imagination.

His hips flexed under her palms, power undulating with every thrust. Fascinated, she turned to the side to watch in the mirrors. It took her breath away. If watching his body work as he fought turned her on, this might just kill her. The single hottest sight she'd ever witnessed.

Rich caught her. "Changed your tune?" he teased, words stilted.

She met his gaze, smiling. "Maybe."

"What else you wanna see?"

Unsure what he meant, she didn't answer. As though punishing her for her hesitance, he pulled out, scooting back on his knees. "Turn over."

At once nervous and intrigued, she did. Rich adjusted her so they were in three-quarters profile to the mirror. He looked even more intimidating this way, torso erect, face cast down at her body. He stroked her waist and hips, then guided himself between her thighs, sliding deep with a long moan.

She watched him, and he watched her in return, until finally their eyes met in the reflection. Heat flashed between them. This position that had always equaled blind surrender to Lindsey became something more. Something equitable and shared, no matter that he was above her, behind her, in control of the motions. Able to watch, she suddenly knew this was for her, every bit as much as it was for him.

And Jesus, he looked amazing.

His hands floated above her skin, the barest whisper. Then he held her, fingers digging gently. Her softer areas jiggled from the impact, but she could tell this sensation that normally embarrassed her was exciting Rich. She wasted time worrying about these things, when in reality her so-called imperfections turned him on.

"You're so sexy," he muttered, gaze jumping between her body and its reflection.

She was ready to respond, but the words fled as he wrapped his arm around her waist, fingertips grazing her clit.

"Oh."

"Tell me what you need."

"Just. That." That, and this view, his voice, those eyes, the weight of his body bumping hers and the stiff length of him, driving deep.

He teased her with one hand, kneading her hip and backside with the other. Every rough thrust, every hard inch, lit her up. As her pleasure grew, she sensed his doing the same. In no time they seemed to be rushing, racing toward the prize. The scene blurred in front of her eyes, all her awareness caught on what he made her feel—served, used, celebrated, desired. Everything, all from a single man. Overcome, she dropped her head and got lost in the impact and friction.

Excitement strained his voice. "You feel so good." His hips sped up, all rhythm lost.

"Rich."

His fingers were shaking, but any pleasure lost was replaced by the thrill of feeling him come apart behind her. The pleasure grew from heat to a taut, physical demand, the need to release bordering on pain.

"Rich. Please."

His fingertips moved with practiced ease and her excitement coiled tighter, tighter, until the sensations burst and flooded, the orgasm leaving her shaking and panting beneath him. His hips hammered her hard for a flurry of thrusts, then he, too, gave in.

She watched his face in the mirrors, all the arrogance gone from those handsome features, desperation and relief uncovered. His eyes shut, he drove deep, the length of his body tensing with a series of grunts before finally going still.

His eyes opened, finding hers. Damp hands slid up her ribs and back, then down again before he secured the condom and eased out.

As he disposed of it, Lindsey collapsed in a happy heap across the comforter. He joined her, pulling her sweaty body close and sighing into her hair, pure male happiness. She sighed right back.

"Damn," he murmured. "Didn't even have to show you my belt."

She reached back to whap his ribs and Rich quit his teasing, feeling familiar and fond as he kissed her jaw.

For ten minutes or more they lay in lazy, companionable silence as their breathing slowed. Lindsey shifted around in his arms to stroke his chest.

"When we were sitting on the fire escape," she murmured, "you looked like some profound thought had struck you."

"Oh?"

"When you were telling me about fighting, and how it makes you feel. Respected, I think you said."

Rich rolled onto his back and swallowed, gaze trained on the ceiling. His fingertips wandered across her belly, but his brain was elsewhere.

"You're doing it now. Your head is someplace else. What is it?"

He met her eyes, expression serious, even vulnerable. "I'd never thought about it like that until I said it. About how it's the only time I feel worthy or whatever. And yeah, respected. And how that's what… That was what wrecked my father."

"How so?"

"He was a somebody when he was my age, in Colombia. He taught engineering in Medellín, back in the Escobar days. But he came here, and his experience and skills didn't count for shit. He traded all that so he and my mom, and eventually us kids, could have a safer life. But he never got over that—losing his identity. I know once upon a time he was a great man. But I never got to meet that guy. All I ever got was the ghost haunting our second-floor den."

She sensed there was more and held her tongue.

"I almost get it now. Coming home how I did, feeling stripped of what I can do, and who that makes me. Even with people around you who know your potential and see you the way you were, the way you want to be seen… It's not enough, if you don't feel it about yourself."

"But you'll be that somebody again. You're him *now*. Just minus a foot."

"I know that…but I—" He stopped himself, seeming to hit some invisible wall. "Anyhow. It just made me understand him, for a second."

Clearly, it wasn't a revelation he relished exploring further.

"I don't want to talk about all that, with us finally naked in a bed."

She blushed.

He turned onto his side and kissed her shoulder. "I knew we'd be good together, but I hadn't expected…"

She squeezed his hand at her waist, waiting and hoping to hear the rest of that thought. But in the end, he just laughed soundlessly, smiled and sighed against her neck.

They lay in silence for a time—five minutes, twenty, an hour? Rich's breathing deepened once more, muscles going slack against her as he fell asleep, snoring softly. She cuddled closer, content simply to be sharing this space with him.

Eventually her body cooled and reality intruded, clearing the happy fog from her head and uncovering worries. She gently pulled away, trying and failing not to wake him.

"Don't," he said, clasping her wrist.

"My sister's going to notice I'm gone."

"I have to leave here at five to catch the bus—surely she won't be up by then."

"Well, no."

"Plus, even if she was, she'd know exactly where to find you if she really needed you. Right?"

Her blush returned. "Yes, I suppose she would."

"So stay." He tugged, and she submitted, rolling back against him. Rich made a lazy, triumphant noise, wrapping his arm tight around her middle and kissing her ear.

As nice as the contact was, it was the surprise of his insistence that had her flushed and happy. Even with their mutual itch scratched, he still wanted her close. She wanted the same, though she'd been careful not to let herself expect it would be the case.

But here she was. In Rich Estrada's bed. The man she'd obsessed over for ten months straight and whose career she'd stalked with the fervor of a teenage superfan. But that wasn't the man she'd just made love to.

No swaggery facade. Not a celebrity or even the man she'd been so infatuated with, but a friend. A friend who happened to have a cage fighter's body, granted, but she'd connected with so much more than his physique or persona. This was a man those women on the message boards could never hope to meet, or likely care to. A human being, as fragile as he was strong. Surely a fact he'd never admit aloud, but the helpless look in his eyes, the trembling in his arms as they made love, the need in his voice when he'd asked her to stay...

She knew this man, in some way she couldn't articulate.

And she knew, as well, she was in deep trouble.

10

For a long time after they crawled under the covers and Lindsey dropped off to sleep, Rich held her. He listened to her breathing, felt the faint muscle twitches as she dreamed, reveled in her warmth.

He ought to be dead asleep, conked by his orgasm. But a restlessness kept him alert, a sensation like the one he sometimes got from his broken foot, a fidgetiness deep beneath the plaster and skin.

He'd never had sex like that.

Well, mechanically he'd had sex pretty much every way there was, but still—nothing like that.

It was as though Lindsey had used that trick of hers—used her eyes to crack his heart open like a piñata so all his emotions tumbled out onto her lap. Except this time she'd used her hands and voice and the warmest, sweetest shadows of her body, and the way it made him feel was all the more intense.

It scared him. It made him wish he were the one being held, so that maybe this unnerving, exposed sensation would ease.

It scared him…but he liked it. Nowhere else in his world would he make room for this feeling. Not in the ring, not in front of his guy friends, not even with his family. His mom and sister were stuck with him during his good spells and bad ones, but Lindsey…she could see through the man he presented to the world, stared through that mask to the uncertainty and the dark thoughts and the loneliness, and she wanted him anyway. He swallowed, throat tight.

He remembered her news, that article she was going to do: Boston's Most Eligible Bachelorette. For the first time in ages, jealousy registered. Rich didn't get attached to women—not enough to feel this ugly, hot sensation licking at the back of his neck. But dumb as the impulse was, he didn't want Lindsey advertised as a single woman. He didn't want hundreds of men's eyes on her on a magazine cover. He wanted her right here. *His*. But that wasn't something he could ever ask for, not when he wasn't willing or able to offer it in return. Or brave enough to even admit it out loud.

Emotion was welling in him, a deep and expanding mass, more than he knew what to do with. But his brain didn't need to know how to handle it—his body had the answer. And that answer lay in his arms.

"Linds." He rubbed her neck with his nose and whispered a little louder. "Lindsey."

"Mmm."

He urged her to turn. When she was on her back, he straddled her beneath the covers, arousal already sharpening at feeling her bare skin on his, cock growing stiff against her hip. He lowered himself and kissed her collarbone and shoulders, waiting for signs that she wanted what he did, for the sexy, rasping way she breathed when she got excited, the strokes of her curious hands. After a minute's soft kisses he was rewarded with a low, hot sigh and the drag of her fingertips down his back.

"I want you," he murmured.

She made a noise, an amused *hmm*. "You just had me."

"I need you. Are you too sore?"

She stroked his hair. "No. I'm fine."

He pushed up on straight arms and stared at her face in the low light. "I'll be gentle." Not as a favor, either. It was what he craved right now—to go slowly and deep and savor every second.

She smiled. "Be however you want."

He left her to don a condom and wet his fingers with lube, then settled between her thighs, finding and parting her lips, gently slicking them with his fingertips. He stroked himself with the excess and angled his crown to her heat, pushing in slowly, slowly, slowly.

The hands on his shoulders tensed along with her breath, then she softened as he eased past a point of resistance.

"Okay?" Jesus, he sounded as if they were losing their virginity together. Felt like that, though. As if he was about to do something he never had before, something profound that would change who he was.

"You feel good," she assured him, smiling and grazing her palms over his face, down his neck, his chest. Her legs hugged his waist.

Then Rich did something he never had before. He reached back and pulled the covers over them.

That was how people had sex on TV and in boring romantic movies—under the blankets. Nobody did that in real life, did they? Why would you? It covered up all the good stuff.

But right now he didn't care about the view. He just wanted to feel wrapped up with her. Inside her, against her. He looked in her eyes and felt that scary magnetism as she dragged the sincerity and insecurity right out of him, and he didn't fight it. He let the awe wash through him in waves, let it rock him, let it make a sloppy lover of him for a minute or two, until he found a balance. He did exactly what his body asked. His strokes were tight and graceless, surely not much to look at, had the covers been shed, but none of that mattered. All that mattered was that he was here, in his bed, being offered Lindsey's warm body, with those eyes bearing witness.

Soon enough, she went from welcoming to something else—piqued and antsy.

"Tell me what you need," he said.

"Can I be on top?"

"Of course." Yes, good. If she was going to make a vulnerable mess of him, let her drive. Let her own his body the way she seemed to possess his mind.

They turned over, Lindsey straddling, covers slipping to her waist. She moved against him as she had that night in the gym, with short, muscular strokes that built friction between the root of his cock and her clit. Hypnotized, he held her thighs, rubbing with his thumbs. Her hair slipped from behind her ear, glowing golden in the light from the hall, casting her face in a shadow. Like some devious sex angel sent from heaven or hell to test him or reward him or God knew what.

There was so much he wanted to say. *No one's ever made me feel this. What the hell have you done to me? Does this feel special to you? Can you hear me thinking all this stuff? Are we making love? Is that even a thing?*

But uttering those thoughts would take far more courage than stripping down and offering another man the chance to draw Rich's blood with an audience of millions. He let his body speak. Let her see the way his hands trembled and his hips shifted, all this evidence of what she did to him. What this felt like…

Surrender.

It was too foreign a concept to wrap his mind around. He shut his eyes and ground his head into the pillow, arched his back, gave himself over to her purposes.

When he knew she was close, he turned them onto their sides, legs tangling. Their lips touching, eyes open, he slipped a hand between their bellies, teasing her clit until she cried out, shuddering against him. He chased her with a dozen quick, shallow thrusts, falling into an orgasm as long and sweet and exquisite as he'd ever felt, a perfect and pleasurable collapse, his world crumbling to pieces as her name fled his lips. She held his head, her palms covering his ears so it echoed in his head like a secret.

Lindsey...

THE NEWS CAME Monday morning.

Rich was just logging on to the gym's computer system, having promised Mercer he'd take on the annoying task of calling to harangue MIA members.

"I'm about as enticing as a schoolmarm," Mercer had said. "But if Rich Estrada tells people to get off their asses and come for a session, they will."

Normally, he'd dread the assignment, but today...

Nothing could touch him today. Not with memories of his night with Lindsey pleasantly clouding his mind and body. He was so...relaxed. As relaxed as he liked for the world to believe he always felt, but so rarely did for real.

His phone buzzed and he checked the screen. Those other calls would have to wait.

He hit Talk. "Chris."

"Rich, hey." His manager's voice filled him with a mix of curiosity and fear. He hadn't been expecting a chat.

"Bit early in San Diego to be checking up on me, isn't it?"

"Maybe, but I've been in Vegas all weekend and I have absolutely no clue what time it is anymore. But if *you're* awake, I got news."

"Wide-awake. Whatcha got for me?"

"So I met with the big man, and we've been talking about you." The big man could mean only one person—the president of the MMA organization Rich fought for. "Got a present for you, bro."

"Who?"

"Vicente Farreira, if you want him."

"Whoa."

Farreira had been a big deal a while back—the org's heavy-weight champ for the better half of a year. He'd ripped a ten-don and gone quiet for a time, but he was only thirty-three or four, still ripe for a comeback, with a massive Brazilian following.

"If I want *him?* Does he want me?"

"Apparently his rehab's done and he's slimmed down, and he wants a new belt. Yours, to be specific. And he wants… Hang on, I can quote it for you." After a pause Chris read, "'I bleeping hate that guy. Every win a bleeping fluke, and I hate his bleeping attitude. He's a bleeping wannabe *Colombiano* and I want to mess up his pretty face and make all the girls cry.'"

"He does want me. How sweet."

And frigging *exciting*. This match would be by far the big-gest promotion, dramawise, that Rich had yet been offered. A comeback title bout with a near legend. Even if he lost, it would propel his career to a new level.

"The org wants this to go down at the biggie event Thanks-giving weekend."

"Oh, shit." That was just over three months away. "You know I got a broken foot, right?"

"I talked to your doc yesterday. He says you're healing right on schedule and that cast can go by mid-September."

"That still only gives me two months to get back in con-dition. Plus Farreira's jujitsu is light-years ahead of mine."

"Last fight before the main event, Rich."

"Goddamn." Too good an opportunity to pass up. And if he did pass it up, he'd lose the respect of the bigwigs. Guys would happily take that fight still wearing a cast. In fact, that's exactly what Rich would've done, had this opportunity come a month ago.

So why was he hesitating now? "Of course I'll take it."

"Excellent."

"I respect that guy's game, but I'll be more than happy to show him whose title that is. How much?"

"Dunno yet. I'm gonna ask for one-fifty."

Rich blinked. A hundred and fifty grand. The figure was so surreal, he couldn't even process how it made him feel. Just…numb. From his head to his shattered foot. "Well, damn."

"Farreira's comeback? It's gonna be a ratings maker. They might drag us down to one even, but I'll see if there's a knockout bonus in it for you. That's your signature, after all."

"And I sure as shit don't want to go to the mat with that guy."

"I don't want that, either, bro."

"You gotta quit calling me bro, Chris. I didn't rush for your frat."

"Anyway. I'll tell the big man you're in, see what kind of payday I can get you. They're gonna want you back in San Diego, stat. I can get you on a plane Wednesday morning, if that works."

"Wednesday. This Wednesday? Two days from now?"

"No time like the present."

"Right." A thought struck Rich like a punch, but it wasn't some vision of pushing too hard and refracturing his foot, or dropping Mercer back in the lurch, or even the look of worry and sadness on his mom's face when he announced he was leaving again. It was a flash of that heat he felt every time Lindsey smiled at him. That look, shot from across a room or beamed up at him in bed last night.

He gave his head a shake. "I'll be ready."

They hung up and Rich stared at the computer screen. He felt…concussed.

He scribbled figures on a Post-it note. A hundred grand, minus taxes and Chris's cut… That still left plenty to sock away for Diana's wedding, pad out their emergency fund, maybe even enough to do what Rich had been hoping to, his pipe dream of the past few years. A nice, fat down payment so he could make their aging landlord an offer on the house.

Rough memories or not, that place was where they belonged. Even if Rich could afford to move the Estradas into some giant-ass waterfront McMansion in Manchester-by-the-frigging-Sea, it wouldn't feel like home. Plus the rent on the adjoining units would mean regular income, probably enough to cover his mom's exorbitant health insurance.

It was all happening. Things he'd dreamed about for years. Even sitting here, having just gotten the news that could make it real…

Where elation should have been was emptiness. And when he imagined all those goals accomplished—the deed to the house, his mother's happy tears, his sister's wedding—every box checked that he'd always assumed would make him feel worthy…

The numbness lifted, and beneath it was panic. Everything he wanted was within his grasp, yet all he could imagine was a mountain. He was nearing the final push, but after he reached the peak and thrust his arms into the sky, triumphant, what then? Only the descent. And what lay at the bottom? An absence of debt and stress, yes, but also an absence of purpose. And a long trek down, for the rest of his life.

He could feel the storm clouds gathering now, cold grayness pooling heavily around his shoulders.

LINDSEY WAS A WRECK all morning.

A happy wreck, a jumble of excitement and nerves, tossed

between hope and pragmatism, suspecting last night had meant something, but knowing she'd be foolish to blindly assume Rich agreed.

But it sure had *felt* like something special, and job title aside, Lindsey wasn't a hopeless romantic—not after this past year. She had the odd flash of ridiculous romanticism, of course. And sure, on her train ride into the city, she'd fantasized about Rich winning his next fight, and adding a new name to his thank-yous when the announcer interviewed him, those shoulders still gleaming under the bright lights.

"Thank you, Mamá. Thank you, Diana. Thank you, Lindsey, love of my life."

She had to snort, the vision was so corny. So corny, yet so damned intoxicating.

Their parting that morning had been hazy. She hadn't heard an alarm, and had no time to panic before Rich woke her saying, "I gotta head out." She'd mumbled an "Okay," and he'd kissed her temple and squeezed her knee, adding, "Don't forget your laundry." Then he'd been gone.

For ten minutes she'd rolled this way and that, stretching, marinating in the sheer pleasure of being wound in Rich Estrada's sheets, in his bed, in his room, surrounded by his smell. Then all too soon she'd been wide-awake and feeling silly. She'd dressed quickly and resisted any urges to snoop. The odds were rock-solid she'd find *something* in his drawers or closet that would burst her happy bubble. The room held practically his entire history, and he wasn't exactly a saint. Plus she didn't *want* her bubble burst. She'd spent too long already trying to know the man through secondhand scraps. The only facts she wanted to learn were the truths he murmured against her skin, brash voice rendered soft by intimacy.

I thought about you while I was away.

I knew we'd be good together, but I hadn't expected...

Expected what? Sadly, she wasn't to know.

As Jenna passed her a fresh cup of coffee, she held on to the mug, not letting Lindsey take it yet.

"So?" Jenna said.

"So?"

She gave her very *Jenna* look. "Don't think I can't tell."

"Can't tell what?"

She released the cup. "That something's up with you. Something personal that I'd like to hear about."

Jeez, the woman was like a romance bloodhound. "As my boss, you realize that's a completely inappropriate demand."

"As your friend, I find I don't really care. Just tell me this—is it Rich?"

Lindsey blinked, way too slow in denying anything. Finally she sighed, busted. "That obvious?"

"You guys have a way of…groping each other with your eyes."

"Oh, great. And here I thought I was playing it so incredibly cool."

"Is it serious?"

Was it? Sex-clouded hope was all fine and good, but in reality, he'd be gone in a few months' time. Plus, well… "It's Rich."

"Is it serious to you?"

She deflected further. "No, no. It's just…he's got this, like, waist to hip to butt ratio, you know?"

Jenna laughed. "That he does."

"But no, it's not serious. How could it be when he's only home to convalesce?"

"True." Jenna looked sad, then shrugged it off. Lindsey wished she could shed the melancholy so easily.

"I've been waiting for this," Jenna said. "Ever since you and Brett broke up, I wondered how long until Rich got his way."

She blushed. "Maybe I got *my* way." *Maybe I'd have got-*

ten my way a year ago, if not for your nosy, well-meaning, fling-ruining text message. "But in any case, it is what it is. Don't get all excited and start giving me your used bridal magazines."

Jenna laughed. "I'll do my best to resist."

They settled in to work, but Lindsey couldn't concentrate.

So Jenna thought Lindsey and Rich were obvious. That anybody could see there was something there. And Jenna was trained in these things.

Lindsey tried not to give the idea too much merit. And perhaps wisely so. By eleven-thirty, Rich hadn't stopped by to say hello, and the wait was gnawing on her insides.

Screw it. She'd just have to make first contact herself. It might look eager, but it beat all this waiting.

She took Jenna's lunch order, then headed downstairs. Mercer was on the mats, showing a group of guys some grappling move. She waited until he stood, then caught his eye. "Any requests from the deli?"

"Yeah, please—loaded turkey sub, if you don't mind. Can I pay you later?"

"Sure. Is Rich around?"

"Office."

She made a beeline, hoping she looked casual, though her heart thudded harder with every step.

The door was wide open and Rich was on the phone, expression full of that easy charm.

"Hazard of the job," he told the phone. "Sooner than I'd expected, actually. But no official word yet… Yeah, thanks. So, any chance we can see you down here a little more regularly this fall…?" He spotted Lindsey and held up a finger to say, *Hang on a sec.*

But the conversation seemed likely to go on, so she skirted the desk and on a notepad scribbled, "Anything from the deli?"

Their fingers brushed as he took the pen and replied with "Roast beef on onion roll, thx." He muttered a few *uh-huhs* as he found his wallet and handed Lindsey a twenty, with a little look and nod that said, *That's for yours, too.* She left the office feeling as if the bill was a diamond engagement ring, something obscenely precious clasped in her clammy hand.

When she got back a half hour later, Rich had escaped the office and was loitering by the water cooler on his crutches, a fresh patch of sweat darkening his T-shirt.

But he wasn't talking to one of the usual guys—not a guy, even.

The mystery woman was built as if she'd been cut out of marble, rolled-over drawstring shorts hugging her slim hips, athletic bra doing nothing to hide her improbable abs. She was milk-pale, with freckles on her arms and flushed face, long red hair held back by a bandanna. Rich said something and she laughed, nearly doubling over. She smacked his arm, then grabbed a gym bag from beside the wall, and Rich led her across to the lounge. She disappeared inside, presumably to change, since there wasn't a women's locker room. Not yet.

Lindsey's stomach gave a queasy gurgle. She'd rounded third base with Rich in that room, and a petty bit of her didn't want another woman stripping down in there.

Don't be one of those girls, she scolded herself. *He's not even your boyfriend. Get a grip.* She took a deep breath, willing the heat surely reddening her face to go away. Rich spotted her as she approached.

"Hey, perfect timing!" He took the foil-wrapped sandwich she handed him. "Thanks a bunch. This morning's been nothing but nonstop chaos."

"Who's that you were talking to?" Lindsey asked oh so casually. "Your first official female recruit?"

"No, no. That's Steph Healy. She fights as Penny Healy?" Name recognition dawned. "Oh, I've heard of her. I didn't know what she looked like." In truth, the draw of MMA for Lindsey was 90-plus percent male-physique-based—specifically Rich's physique. She hadn't paid much attention to the few women's matches she'd come across. "She doesn't look like a Penny." *She looks like an assassin.*

"I think it's an old nickname, and not one she's especially fond of. I met her in Vancouver. We worked out together the week before the tournament there. She can sprint a mile in five twenty, if you can believe that." He made a face, clearly impressed.

"Does she have a match coming up around here, or…?"

Rich shook his head. "Mercer talked her into consulting for us, about the best way to make this place coed. And she had a week free, so she agreed to come up and check out what we've got going on."

"I see."

"She's retiring from the circuit soon."

"She looks a bit young to be retiring."

"She's sick of the road. Ready to settle down and start teaching. Mercer thinks he's nearly convinced her to take a job our full-time jujitsu trainer. But it's kind of a task, seducing her away from whatever better offers she's probably got."

Seducing her how, exactly?

"It'll be more attractive to women if we have an established female fighter on hand."

"So were you auditioning her or something? You're all sweaty." She'd seen that face flushed from exertion under quite different circumstances, and arousal momentarily trumped any jealousy she felt.

"Just messing around. She's from a completely martial-arts background, unlike most of us. She wanted to try her hand at a bit of old-school Golden Gloves–style sparring. She's not bad."

"Oh, cool." Yeah, super. Attractive, semi-famous female ass-kicker hanging around the gym running five-minute miles in a sports bra. Lindsey felt herself drifting deeper into the background, the shadows, just like always. Then she remembered the photo shoot invitation. *Bring it on.*

"You don't think that'll be distracting for the guys?"

Rich shrugged. "Good for everyone to get used to working with distractions."

"Yeah, I guess it would be."

"Not a worry for me, anyhow," Rich added. "I won't go near Irish girls. They're nuts, every last one of them."

Lindsey's hope perked back up from its defeated heap. "That's a bit racist."

"Trust me, they're crazy. Add that to the fact that the girl fights?" He shook his head, looking terrified by the thought. "No, thank you. Call me a chauvinist, but I like women with fewer bruises than me. Ones who'll let me wear the pants."

Lindsey immediately imagined Rich letting said pants drop to the floor.

"I like wearing pants," she said, glancing down at her trousers.

"And they look lovely."

Not as lovely as I'll look on the cover of a magazine. How might they style her? She'd insist on a skirt, at the very least. And very girly shoes. Shoes she'd never dare attempt actually walking in. Shoes she'd leave on should the cover inspire Rich to toss her onto the nearest flat surface and have his way with her pantslessness.

He looked suddenly uncomfortable, toying with the foil on his sandwich. "I, uh, got some interesting news today."

"What kind of news?"

"I can't say too much about it until some ink dries, but go with me for a coffee after the lunchtime rush and I'll let you in on the gist."

She considered her schedule. "I'm flexible between two and three."

"Perfect. Meet me in the foyer at two-fifteen."

After a couple of restless hours, she did, and they walked a few blocks to a coffee shop. She was torn—excited for this date, if that's what it was, but nervous about what his cagey tone might mean.

"Tell me what you want and I'll carry everything over," she offered.

He scanned the chalkboard above the counter. "Uh, the thing that's got foam, but less foam than the really foamy thing?"

"A latte?"

"With low-fat milk. No sugar."

Lindsey placed their orders and carried them to the window table Rich had snagged. The afternoon sun was bright, lighting up his eyes. His irises were so dark they often looked black, but the sunlight revealed a rainbow of warm browns.

"Thanks." He reached for his wallet but she waved it away.

"My treat. Thanks for lunch." Oh, goodness, this all sounded so…couple-ish. "So what's this big news?"

He stirred his latte, eyes on the task. "My manager called. The guys up top want me to fight Vicente Farreira."

"Whoa."

"You know who he is?"

"Yeah, I've seen his name around. He used to be a huge deal, right? Where'd he go?"

"Nasty injury, plus he lost his title, so maybe a bit of a sulking spell. His camp's real secretive. But apparently he hates my guts, and he's dying for a chance to break my face and steal my belt."

"Wow. And you're going to do it?"

"Can't pass up a big-deal fight like that. Second billing.

And if I can manage to win, no way my next match won't be the main event."

"Oh, my. That's, like, crazy-exciting. Should we be horrible employees and buy a bottle of champagne on the way back?"

He laughed. "My drinking days are numbered. The fight's scheduled for the last week of November."

"Damn, that's soon."

"No kidding. They want me back in California on Wednesday to start training."

A dull, psychic thump knocked Lindsey in the head.

Rich kept talking, something about Farreira and Brazilian jujitsu and needing to buckle down, but she caught only every fifth word.

Wednesday.

She'd known he'd be gone eventually…but she'd thought she might not have to actually accept that until the fall.

He drained his cup. "I better get back. Your sister's got the day off, which means ol' peg-leg has that much more grunt work to do."

Lindsey finished her drink, knowing she'd regret the caffeine. Her nerves were already buzzing, a million panicky ants marching through her veins. God help whatever advice she gave her three-thirty client.

As they left, the August heat and sunshine enveloped Lindsey in a warmth she barely felt. They made their way back toward Chinatown, and too shaken to muster a proper conversation, she lobbed a hundred questions at Rich about the match, *mmm-hmm*ing to keep him talking, keep her attention off the pain in her chest…though that was no use.

If you didn't have those crutches, she wanted to ask, *would you be holding my hand?* She'd never find out now. By the time he ditched them, he'd already have been gone a month. If any girl got her hand held as she strolled down a sidewalk with Rich Estrada—or down a hotel corridor en route to his room, for that matter—it wouldn't be Lindsey.

Panic rose with every step. Scared she might wind up crying, she decided to make a run for it.

She interrupted his dissection of Vicente Farreira's stand-up game. "Crap—I forgot I needed to swing by the drugstore. I'll see you around later?"

He nodded. "Hey, thanks for coming out. I'm glad I got to tell you. I would've exploded, trying to keep that all to myself."

Don't, please. Don't make me feel special.

With a pair of goodbyes, they went their separate ways. Half a block on, Lindsey stopped and turned, watching his back move farther and farther away with every plant of his crutches, feeling her heart grow harder, a tiny fist drawn tight and gnarled as a peach pit.

"Sorry," she muttered as pedestrians altered their courses to get around her. She tucked herself against the building at her back, watching Rich get smaller, smaller.

"Oh, shit." She blinked, realization dawning with sickening clarity as his red shirt disappeared around the corner.

"I'm in love with a frigging cage fighter."

11

"WHAT?" MAYA'S EYES were round as coasters. "He can't do that!"

They were in the kitchen, Lindsey stirring the leftover chili she was heating up for their dinner. She'd known her sister wouldn't take the news of Rich's imminent departure well.

"He's got a chance for a really big-deal fight. He has to get back to San Diego and train his butt off."

"What about us?"

A shrug was all Lindsey could muster, a limp imitation of apathy and acceptance when all she wanted to do was scream. "Rich doesn't owe us anything. And I'm sure if he hadn't gotten this opportunity, he'd be happy to keep training you through the month. And don't forget—Mercer said he'd work with you."

"It's not the same!"

No, it wasn't. "I'm sorry, but that's how it is." It was a truth Lindsey needed to accept, too, even as her exciting new reality fell to pieces around her.

Maya slumped against the counter. "He promised he'd work with me until September. We made a *deal*."

"I don't know what else to tell you. Sometimes we have to leave important things behind, when even more important ones are at stake. Just like you have to put training on hold when school starts."

Maya offered a joyless, disbelieving laugh. "Oh, I am *not* going back now."

Lindsey countered with her best leveling stare.

"No way. Rich was, like, the only teacher I've ever had who made me feel like I was special at something. No *way* I'm going back. They'll probably be happy I don't. One less crappy score messing up their stupid standardized tests and making the school look bad—"

"I'm ending this discussion," Lindsey said. "We can talk more about it when you've calmed down."

"Fine," she snapped. "*Fine.* He just better not be smiling when I show up for my lesson tomorrow, thinking it's cool to just—"

"You should find out if it's still on. God knows what stuff Rich has to run around and get done."

"What? He's just going to brush me off?"

She abandoned the chili, turning to hold Maya's shoulders. "Seriously, chill out. You can't take it personally."

Yet personal was so exactly how it felt to Lindsey. Her brain knew it wasn't, but her heart was ripped and ragged. She'd been left behind for better things before. Brett's abandonment had happened in slow motion, but the pain stayed the same—only concentrated this time around.

Maya slipped out of Lindsey's hold. "I'm going to my room until dinner."

"Fine."

After her sister left, Lindsey leaned into the counter, succumbing to a bone-rattling sigh. Some damage control was needed, lest Rich get blindsided by a tornado of teenage outrage tomorrow at the gym. She turned the burner down and found her phone.

He didn't answer, and when the beep prompted her to

speak she ended the call, throat too tight, mind a blank. Five minutes later her phone jingled, Rich's name on the screen.

"Hi," she said, hearing shouts and bass in the background, the unmistakable soundtrack of the gym.

"You just call?"

"Yes, with a bit of a heads-up. I just broke it to Maya you're going back west, and to say she took it poorly is the understatement of the year."

"Shit. I hadn't even thought that far ahead. But I'm heading out now—I'll swing by when I get home, if you think that'll help."

"Probably better than suffering her tantrum in the gym with all those witnesses."

"No doubt. I'll bring a mouth guard in case it gets ugly."

"See you in a bit."

She didn't bother telling her sister he was coming—it'd only give her a chance to rehearse her diatribe. They were just ladling chili into bowls when the knock came at the door.

Maya's eyes narrowed. "That better not be him."

Lindsey headed for the door, shocked as always by the size of him, the way his face made her IQ drop fifty points. "Hey. Brace yourself."

Rich smiled and hopped inside, spotting Maya at the table. "Hey, kid."

She glared daggers at him. "Hey, traitor."

He made his way over, flipping a chair around and sitting. Lindsey took his crutches and leaned them against the wall, then settled down with her own bowl.

"Traitor, huh? I knew you'd make a good fighter. Fans love a grudge match."

Maya kept on glaring as she blew at her steaming chili.

"Look, kid—"

"Quit calling me kid."

"Sorry. Maya. But listen—I'd happily keep working with

you, if this thing hadn't come up. But you have to admit, if somebody offered *you* a hundred grand to drop everything and give up the next three months of your life...tell me you wouldn't do it."

She couldn't tell him a thing—the figure had struck her dumb.

"But you must get Christmas break, right? We can pick up where we're leaving off when I come home."

The shock faded, her anger returning, but diminished. "I'll have forgotten everything I've learned by then."

"Well, that's your fault, if you don't practice."

"No, it's your fault. For promising something, then going back on it."

"I'm sorry. This is my job, and I have to earn that money for my family. We don't have a dad like you guys do. Okay? I never meant to let you down, but it's not like I'm the only trainer out there."

"You're the only one who'd ever see anything in *me,*" Maya said.

"That's not true. Plus, I promise you, I'm the worst trainer Wilinski's has. You'll be in way better hands with Merce or any of those other guys the next couple weeks."

But Lindsey was on Maya's side on this one. Rich was irreplaceable.

"It's not the same," Maya said, but the passion had gone out of her voice.

Lindsey had to wonder exactly what breed of attachment had her sister so upset. Not a starry-eyed crush, she didn't think, nothing romantic or physical. It had to be that Rich was the one who'd discovered her, in a way. The first authority figure—the first cool adult, for that matter—who thought she was special. Not a father figure, not even a fun older brother. But a successful, talented stranger who had absolutely *no reason* to invest his time or energy being kind to her, but had chosen to anyway. It broke Lindsey's heart to fully appreciate what this meant to her sister.

Rich raked his hands through his hair. "I don't know what to tell you. This is the biggest thing that's ever happened to me."

"Me, too," she muttered, and stood with a squeak of her chair. She left the room and Lindsey put a hand to Rich's forearm to tell him to let her go.

After Maya's door slammed, Lindsey registered the warm muscle under her fingers and pulled them away. "She'll calm down. She got to vent how she was feeling, which is the important thing."

He shrugged. "If she decides to come for a final lesson, I'm happy to let her pummel me, if that helps."

"Want some chili? We've got loads."

"Thanks, but no." He got uneasily to his feet and Lindsey fetched his crutches. "My mom has something in the oven. And I've got to break the news to her and Diana still."

"Oh, right. Won't they be happy?"

"Diana will be, for both the money and because she gets that this is my thing. My mom'll be stressed. And bummed, since she's been so excited to have me home." He headed for the door and Lindsey opened it. "It's like a deployment. She gets that I need to do it, but she still hates that it means I'll be away for months at a time, risking bodily harm. And two days is, like, no warning at all. The rosary's in for a hell of a workout tonight."

"Good luck."

"Once all the weeping and praying's done, odds are twenty to one the next order of business'll be planning a going-away dinner for tomorrow night. Consider yourselves invited."

"Thanks."

They both paused, and it drove home to Lindsey just exactly what they were to each other—friends. With benefits, sure, but friends at the end of the day.

I'm upset, too, she longed to confess. Maya's meltdown embodied everything Lindsey felt about Rich's departure but couldn't be said. *My heart hurts. At least let me sleep next to you one more time. Let me memorize every second with your arms wrapped around me.*

She'd let herself believe she'd have more chances, enough chances for their infatuation to run its course and lose its fire, dull this pain when Rich inevitably left. But he'd be gone in two days, not two months, and she was still smoldering.

Rich put his hand to her jaw, stroked her cheek with an apology in his eyes. For her? For Maya? She felt tears brewing and panicked, pulling away with a burning face. "I'll see you tomorrow."

He straightened, offering a weak smile. "You better."

Already her chin was trembling, and she backed away, praying he couldn't tell. "Congrats again."

Another smile, one Lindsey didn't entirely buy, and he hopped around to begin the awkward trip down the steps.

The tears were falling before she even got the door shut. She emptied Maya's untouched bowl back into the pot, then her own. Apparently, nobody felt much like chili tonight.

IT TOOK EVERY scrap of enthusiasm Lindsey could fake to smile when Lorena opened the door the next evening.

"Welcome, girls." She eyed the Tupperware container of cupcakes Lindsey held. "Aren't you sweet?" She swept them into the kitchen.

Diana was setting the table, Andre rinsing salad greens in the sink. Their greetings didn't hang heavily with the angst Lindsey felt. To them, this going-away party had its emphasis on *party*. But all Lindsey could seem to focus on was the *going-away*. Far away. For months.

It's good, she told herself. *If you really loved him, you'd be happy for him.* As it was, she couldn't help but feel bad for what she was losing. *It's not love,* she promised herself. *Not love, not love.*

"Where's Rich?" Maya asked.

"Destinking himself," Diana said. "Takes him forever with that stupid cast."

He made his appearance shortly, hopping into the kitchen, hair wet and gleaming. "Smells good."

His mother fussed until he made it onto a chair. Rich shot Lindsey and Maya a nervous smile, and rightfully so. He'd had to cancel Maya's lesson and Lindsey hadn't spotted him around the building all day. The last time he'd seen them he'd been gifted with a tantrum and thoroughly half-assed congratulations. Such excellent thanks after he'd found Lindsey a home and given up his free time to work with her sister. *Well done, Tuttles.*

Lindsey dug deep and offered a genuine smile.

While the others were heaping plates, she touched his shoulder and said, "Sorry about last night."

"What about it?"

"You know." She nodded to Maya. "I shouldn't have asked you to come and put out my fires when you're bound to be so busy."

He waved the thought aside. "I started that fire. Wouldn't be fair to leave you on your own with it."

His mother set a plate in front of him, and Lindsey went to assemble her own dinner. She wasn't sure what the main dish was, aside from looking a bit like paella and smelling divine. As she sat, she glanced around the table, wondering if anyone suspected what had gone on upstairs after the last dinner they'd been invited to. How soundproof was this place? She blushed, thankful everyone was preoccupied, passing condiments and raving over their first bites.

Dinner passed in a flurry of questions about Rich's match and training regimen, fretful and excited alike.

"Enjoy this now," Diana teased. "No way they're letting you anywhere near a plate of *arroz marinero* until your fight's over."

"Don't remind me."

"I'll text you photos of Thanksgiving dinner," she added. "To inspire you before your weigh-in."

"If you do, you're out of my thank-you spiel."

She stuck her tongue out at him, and the conversation shifted to Andre's upcoming job interview at the local radio station.

Soon enough, second helpings and cupcakes had been consumed, and the dishes were rinsed and loaded. Diana and Andre excused themselves to watch a show in the living room, and Lorena bade everyone good-night, with a nagging reminder for Rich to be up early for his flight.

Maya had chilled out during the meal, but she was still mired largely in her own disappointment. She cast Lindsey and Rich a look, one that said she understood Lindsey's farewell wasn't something requiring witnesses.

"Thanks," she said to Rich, and let him hug her with a stooped tangle of crutches. "It was cool of you to work with me as much as you did."

"Wish I could've seen you through to September."

"I'll probably live. Have a safe flight."

He flicked her temple and she scowled, then held up her guard with a grudging smile and headed for the door. "You better win or I'll be pissed," she added over her shoulder. Then to Lindsey, "I'm stealing your computer, okay?"

"Color me shocked. I'll be up in a minute."

Then the door shut behind Maya, and it was just the two of them.

Rich grinned and asked, "Only a minute? That bodes poorly for either my chances or my longevity."

She laughed, cheeks heating, the sudden flirtation throwing her for a fresh loop.

"I'm sorry about last night, too," he added quietly. "I'd have asked if you wanted to hang out, but…"

"You had some major news to break to your mom."

"But I'm all packed now, if you felt like having a good-bye drink…?"

Did she?

An invitation to one last taste of their addictive chemistry, a hard offer to pass up. But also an invitation to let Rich burrow that much deeper under her skin, make their actual parting sting all the more. Her obsessive crush had dogged her for ten months the last time he'd gone away. This time she'd be saying goodbye to a friend and lover, not just a hot acquaintance. Every resulting emotion was bound to ache a hundred times worse—longing, jealousy, uncertainty…

But one look at the hopeful, mischievous gleam in those dark eyes, and she knew her answer.

"Sure. That'd be nice." *Yeah, nice. Nice and masochistic.*

They made their way up to Rich's floor, pausing in his kitchen to grab a pair of beers.

"My last drink till Thanksgiving." He smiled, handing her both bottles. "Would you like to see my belt?"

She laughed. "I would, actually."

He led her down the hall. "Oldest trick in the book."

"Funny how you didn't need it last time."

He flipped on his bedroom light and ditched the crutches, hopping to the corner beside his closet. From a flat cardboard box he lifted the belt from between sheets of bubble wrap. Lindsey's eyes grew wide and she set the beers on his dresser, crossing the room.

"Wow, it's heavy." A black-leather-and-gold-plated monstrosity, all done up with rivets, the organization's logo on an octagonal field of chain-link pattern. "Can I try it on?"

"You can wear it to bed for all I care. In fact…" His eyes glazed, suggesting he was imagining her wearing nothing *but* the belt to bed.

She rolled her eyes and wrapped it around her waist, holding it in place as she went to the wall of mirrors.

"Wow, I look tough." She swiveled this way and that, watching the gold glint. "And it's so slimming."

"I wish I could've shown my sixteen-year-old self this. Some hot blonde in my room, modeling my championship belt."

Lindsey did her best cheesy impression of a ring girl, holding the belt aloft and grinning sex-beams all around the room.

"Okay, okay. It's going to your head." He took the belt from her with a smile, nesting it back inside its bubble wrap.

"Do you have to give it back if somebody beats you?"

"No. That'd be kinda gross, considering how many dudes' sweat and blood it'd get marinated in."

"Ew."

He grabbed his beer and hopped to sit on the mattress and unlace his shoe. Lindsey followed suit.

They sat cross-legged, sipping their drinks and talking about the fight for a long time. Then Rich shot her a look, dark with bad intentions.

"What?" she asked, knowing perfectly well *what*. He took her bottle and set it with his on the bedside table. Her middle gurgled with those nerves it seemed she'd never stop feeling, no matter how many times she got close to this man.

Rich lay down, urging her to join him. He sandwiched her knee between his, smiling as he brushed her hair from her face. His gaze jumped from her eyes to her mouth and back again, half a dozen times before he finally leaned in to kiss her. The contact warmed her from her head through her middle, all the way to her toes and fingertips. More than lust, it was the familiarity of this touch, this mouth, this man that had her entire body blushing. She curled her fingers around his collar and deepened the kiss.

Rich tugged her into the embrace, hugging her leg between his thighs. A strong hand molded to her waist, coaxing her center closer to his. Everything that had happened the last time they shared this bed flashed through her memory, sped through her bloodstream. But behind the arousal, a storm cloud lurked.

This is goodbye. No matter how good it is, you might never enjoy it again. And in a few short hours, Rich wouldn't be this man in her arms. He'd be that face on a screen, belonging to everyone.

His hands were at her hem, sliding her top up. She pushed the painful thoughts aside and helped him peel it away. He did the same, and for blissful minutes she got lost in his mouth and the sensation of his restless flesh warming hers. She felt him smile against her lips, heard that smug, happy hum in his throat.

Some other woman could be relishing that same sound, and who knows how soon? Could be tasting this mouth, feeling these hands on her bare skin.

The worries set snakes loose in her belly, twisting queasily.

Rich's fingers found the button of her jeans. She let him lower her fly and ease his palm inside to knead her hip. Eager, he took her hand, pressing it to the front of his pants to find his cock stiff and ready behind the smooth fabric. He slid his hand back inside her jeans to return the caress, and for a minute she was too turned on to feel anything aside from desire.

Then a helpless, hungry moan fell from his lips to warm hers, and the reality of what she was doing—and what she stood to lose—hit home.

Another moan, and he murmured, "I'm going to miss this so much more than beer and ribs."

She went rigid against him, her hand fleeing to his hip.

"There's so much I wanted to do with you," he whispered. "I thought we'd have weeks."

Her voice quavered. "Me, too."

His fingers stroked her, slick and eager. "Before I go…I have to know how you taste." He began edging down her body. "If you'll let me."

"I…"

Noticing she'd gone stiff as stone, he paused and met her eyes. "You okay?"

"I don't know."

"We don't have to, I just like it. But if you—"

She pulled away, feeling naked.

"What's the matter?"

"I can't do this."

RICH SAT UP as Lindsey did the same, dizzy as his body tried to flip so quickly from lust to alarm. His cock ached, angry. But even addled with arousal, he could guess exactly when he'd stepped in it.

Smooth one, jackass.

"Linds, wait. I'm sorry—I was kidding, about the ribs and beer. I'm not really rounding you in with that stuff."

She yanked her top back on. "I know. It's not that."

"What, then?"

She swallowed, meeting his eyes. "I thought I could just roll with this, like it's just fun to me—just sex. But I can't. I'm sorry."

He slung his bad leg over the edge of the bed as Lindsey scrambled for her socks and shoes. "Hey, hey. Slow down."

She studied him as she buttoned and zipped her jeans, some mix of hesitance and resignation in her eyes.

He patted the comforter. "C'mere."

She sat. "Sorry. This was all supposed to be really simple, just the two of us hooking up."

"But it's not?"

"Not to me," she said, eyes on the blanket, then she sighed. "I wanted it to be."

What had it been to him? he had to wonder. A pleasant diversion, to start. A mutually pleasurable arrangement, and one he got to share with a woman he now saw as a friend—not usually how sex worked for him. If it was something more, he couldn't afford to let himself think about it. This time tomorrow, he'd be three thousand miles away. It was a nonoption for too many reasons.

Was he supposed to touch her? Hold her? Unsure, he reached out to rub her knuckles with his fingertips, all the closeness he dared hazard. "What is it for you?"

"I'm not sure. A crush, I guess." This woman, always ready with a barbed retort, yet the admission had her bashful and mumbling. "A bad one. One that gets worse every time we...you know."

That, he understood. The sex should have quenched their thirst for one another, but even he could admit that it only deepened the craving. "Right."

"And as much I want to, I dunno...make the most of you while you're here...it's making it worse. I want way more than you can give me." She paused, huffing a frustrated breath. "Sorry. I didn't want to ever have this conversation with you."

"How come?"

"The same reason it hurts so bad now. Because I knew the score, and I thought I was fine with it being whatever it was, just temporary. And knowing that was supposed to keep me from getting emotional about it. About you."

If someone had given Rich a heads-up about this discussion, he'd have gone into it with dread, formulating a plan to cut her loose as painlessly as possible. *It's not you, it's me.* Which was exactly true, come to think of it. Lindsey was great. She was wonderful. And she deserved a guy who could offer what she herself was prepared to give.

He cleared his throat. "I can't be that for you. Anything more than this," he added, nodding to mean the bed. Never had words left his mouth and made his chest hurt so acutely. Was this guilt? It didn't feel like guilt.

"I know you can't. I knew going in. That's why I feel so stupid for even being upset. You were supposed to leave thinking I was as blasé about our hooking up as you are."

Not guilt, he realized—grief. *I can't be that for you.* It was the truth, but he wished it wasn't.

Rich bit his tongue, so close to admitting it was different for him, as well. But that was a luxury he couldn't afford. "If I come off like I don't care, it's nothing personal. I can't be anything extra to anybody at this point in my life—not aside from my family. I can't make room for anything else, not until I know I've done my job as a provider."

Her smile was limp and void of surprise, twisting his aching heart. "And when will you feel like you've succeeded at that?"

The question spurred a different pang. "I'll just know. I'll know when I've done enough that I can make room for other things. Other people." He had to believe that.

She cast her eyes down and took a deep breath.

"Sorry," he offered, rubbing the back of her hand.

"Don't be sorry. I'm not sad for myself, not beyond feeling really dumb. Not the way I feel sad for you."

"For me?"

"It sounds so…lonely. Only letting yourself be one thing. Like you're hiding behind your role as a provider."

A new feeling surged, one that jabbed with a hot, sharp finger. *Hiding. Lonely.* Rich knew isolation. His father had modeled it for him perfectly. "I'm not hiding from anything. I'm stepping up and doing what needs to be done. I'm not *hiding*." So why on earth would the allegation sting the way it did?

Lindsey's hand slipped from his as she stood. "You're cheating yourself, acting like you've only got one dimension." She hopped, pulling on a sock.

"Has it never occurred to you that maybe I do? I'm good at *exactly* one thing."

She gave him a long, peculiar look, as if translating what he'd said from another language. "There's a lot more to you than that. And it hurts to hear you say the opposite, since that means you must think I was only ever interested in you because of your job or your money—"

"Linds."

"Because it was never about that for me."

What *had* it been for her at the start? Sex? Surely not— Lindsey struck him as too complex a woman for such a simple answer. "What then?"

"I guess…just you."

"What do you mean?"

She sat and pulled on the other sock, thinking. "If I needed anything from you…I don't know what to call it. But it's not something that could be taken away by an injury or a loss."

The words jabbed him anew, discomfort churning.

"It was how you made me feel, maybe. When it was just us, just being with each other. There's this fire in you. This… energy. This thing that made me forget who you were, outside the body in my arms, or the man standing across the room from me." All at once she looked mortified again.

Rich didn't know what to say—he wasn't even 1 percent as good as she was with all this emotional, self-awareness stuff. He needed labels, simple names to assign to who he was and what he felt. Angry, horny, triumphant, exhausted.

Tidy, black-and-white terms that reduced his emotions to on-off switches.

She sighed. "I get that we see the world differently. I'm not trying to get you to change your mind, or saying you should. I guess I just want to say, don't sell yourself short. You've got more to offer than the things you give yourself credit for. And you deserve to feel valued for those things."

Nobody ever said stuff like this to Rich, no one except his mom and sister. The women who knew him. He felt a bone-deep shiver and had to look away from those searching blue eyes. How she managed to peer right through his skin and into his heart, he'd never know. And it was yet another unnamed sensation he couldn't handle right now.

"Anyway," she said, slipping into her shoes.

He opened his mouth but nothing came out. Only one thought wanted to be aired, but he couldn't go there.

Are you in love with me?

Even if she was, Rich would have no clue what to do with it.

He'd been told that by women before. Tipsy women, more often than not, with that starstruck heat in their eyes, right before or after he took them to bed to cap off a fight. That shallow adoration. *I think I might love you,* he'd been told, and he'd smiled as if he believed it. But in his brain, all that echoed was *You don't know the first thing about me. About who I am, where I'm from, what matters to me, what goes through my head before I fall asleep. You don't love me. You haven't even met me.* But he let them believe they did. Let himself believe it for as long as it took to bed them, because the truth was too lonely to contemplate.

But Lindsey.

She *did* know him, as much any lover ever had. And those moments when his walls had slipped and he'd told her things…she *had* actually met him. Peeled him open like a banana, when all these years he'd imagined his defenses were impenetrable.

She offered a weak smile. "Thanks for everything you did for my sister."

"You're welcome."

"I'm sure I'll see you around, next time you're home. Sorry if I just made it awkward."

He froze, throat too tight to reply.

"Have a safe flight." She mustered a smirk, some of the sadness gone. "Kick Farreira's ass."

He returned her smile, but still no words came.

Grab her hand. Pull her back. Kiss her until you know what to say to keep her from going. But the surety that let Rich step nearly naked into a cage…it was nowhere close to the courage he needed now. He let her turn. Let her walk out, watching the shadows in the hall flicker until she'd gone.

A distant squeak, a click and a minute later, muted footsteps above him as Lindsey retired to her own room.

Rich lay back and held his hand up toward the ceiling, opening and closing his fingers. Her body was no more than ten feet from his.

Yet he'd never felt so alone in his entire life.

12

He kissed his mother and sister goodbye outside the terminal, promising to call when he landed in San Diego. His mom had wept the entire drive to Logan, ten miles that felt like fifty between rush-hour traffic and the cloud of Catholic guilt.

A security runaround was inevitable with the crutches and cast, but Rich made it through the gauntlet with time to spare. And as he relaced his sneaker on the other side, he was free.

He sat quietly for a minute, straining to manifest what he ought to be experiencing.

This is where you feel happy, asshole.

Or at least relieved. Grateful to be done with everything except fighting. No coaching, no cleaning, no secretarial duties, no more strangers wanting to rehash the injury with him. He was back to being the center of his own universe, 100 percent focused on the thing he was good at.

Maybe he'd skip the happy relief stage and jump straight into the blind focus. Yeah, that was a plan. No time for excitement—he had to get his head where it needed to be, mind on nothing except the moment he'd be in that ring, staring Farreira dead in the eyes.

He swung toward his gate and fetched a coffee with much

awkward juggling, sipping as he sat and stared out the windows at taxiing planes.

You're the light heavyweight champ. You've got the fight of your life in three months.

You're waiting for a plane to fly you across the country, to Rio come November, and maybe this spring it'll be England or Japan or Australia. This is what you've been dreaming about, the thing thousands of guys would kill for but only a handful ever get.

So why did he feel so…

Empty? Exhausted?

Depressed.

That's the word you can't even bear to utter in your head.

He shut his eyes, leaning back in the seat.

He hadn't felt this last year. But last year he hadn't known what he did now. He hadn't known how much his mother missed him, or indeed exactly how much he'd miss her. He hadn't known he was valuable to Wilinski's as anything more than a body willing to show up at six and do his part. He hadn't realized how much he'd miss the cold bite of winter and the salt crunching under his shoes, or how those skeletal trees were so much more *right* than any swaying palm.

Last year…

He swallowed and opened his eyes, staring at the city skyline. It was just past ten. His heart sped. He felt a weird tug, knowing exactly where she was amid all those buildings. Sitting only a few feet above where he'd spent hours and days and years, nearly two decades. And tonight she'd go to sleep one floor above the room he'd called his nearly his entire life.

She'll still be in those places the next time you touch down.

Likely. She'd still be where he lived, where he worked. But where he felt her was far closer to home. Like a sliver, sharp and barbed, lodged in his heart.

A selfish part of him wished he'd ended things differently.

That he'd let her know she meant something to him. But self-serving as Rich could be, that would've been a step too far. Admit he cared for her as more than a friend or lover, leave her waiting in patient, lonely fidelity. Then come home, pray they hadn't dreamed that connection, then what? Gone again a few weeks later.

She deserved a man who'd put her first. Rich might even have wanted to be that man in some alternate reality where he was free to care. He might have grown to love that scary sensation, the way her eyes cut through his armor to let the anger and fear escape, making room for him to take a deep breath.

But wishing didn't change circumstances. And emotions, unless diligently corralled and harnessed, served only to drag a man down. A legacy he'd sworn never to inherit.

So when boarding commenced and his zone was called, Rich joined the funneling crowd, aware of the curious looks he earned—his build and scars, the crutches and cast hinting at a story he was too weary to recount. He was relieved when no one asked.

His boarding pass was scanned, the young woman on duty flashing him a smile she hadn't gifted his fellow passengers. He returned it, feeling lonelier still as he made his way through the gate.

Self-pity's a luxury, he reminded himself, gaze locked on the next step, the next step. *One you haven't earned yet.*

But a soft, clear voice echoed in a darker corner of his mind, lighting up shadows he preferred not to look upon.

Will you ever feel like you've earned it?

Would the prize money ever feel like enough of a safety net? And what happened when his body simply couldn't do this any longer?

If I needed anything from you…it's not something that could be taken away by an injury or a loss.

What that thing was, Rich had no clue. No clue how to label it, or how to offer it.

And there was no place in his world for anything but the concrete. Money. Contracts. Family duty. The next fighter who stood in Rich's way and the skills to conquer him. Lust and the physical acts that satisfied it.

No shapeless feelings, no indefinable *something*. No ache in his chest or restlessness in his bones from these emotions. Pain only from injury, wounds treated with ice and ointment and time.

He felt too much in Boston.

And the sooner the city slid away beneath him, the sooner he'd remember who he was.

DEAR GOD, WHY had she ever agreed to this?

Lindsey watched the activity swirling around the Spark office from the threshold—assistants moving her and Jenna's desks, adjusting the placement of plants and bookshelves to create the perfect backdrop for Lindsey's photo shoot.

It was Monday and Jenna had closed the office, treating it like a holiday, arriving early to let the magazine people in. She was playing maid of honor in what she kept calling Lindsey's "big day," a hyper bundle of excitement.

In her brain, Lindsey was grateful Jenna was so supportive. But in her heart…

The editor had emailed the cover copy the night before, so Lindsey might "get into the vibe."

Boston's Most Eligible Bachelorette:
Why this matchmaker and wedding planner is in no rush to say "I do."

A couple weeks ago, Lindsey would've been only too happy to play that role. She'd been freshly single and happily so, free to be with Rich after mooning over him for practically a year. Except she'd blinked, and it was over. And after this shoot, she'd head home to a cranky teenage roommate and have to call her parents and report that, if anything, this experiment in Boston living had made things worse, as far as getting Maya back in school went.

"Hi!" A beaming young man with perfectly styled hair swept in from the meeting room, a swath of tulle heaped over his arm. Enthusiasm radiated off him in waves. "You're Lindsey! You're even prettier in person."

"Oh. Thank you." She shook his hand, shoving the worries to the back of her head.

"I'm James, the creative director for this shoot. We are going to have *so much fun*. Are you ready for your cover-model debut?"

"Ready as I'll ever be."

He patted the heap of fabric. "So the visual concept is that you're a fairy godmother to your clients. A young, hip, sexy fairy godmother." He grinned, clearly wanting Lindsey to be equally delighted by this idea.

"That's so cool," she hedged, smiling through her nerves. "But exactly how sexy?"

"Don't worry, not *too* sexy. This isn't a men's magazine."

"Is that a wedding dress?"

"It is!" James unfurled the gown, an outrageous explosion of gauze and crepe and oversize sequins. "Betsey Johnson! Isn't it a scene? Custom couture job, then the wedding gets called off. Her loss, our gain."

"It's very…funky. I love it. But doesn't that contradict the whole concept about me not being in a rush to say 'I do'?"

"We're going to tint it digitally so it won't scream *bridal* in the final image. Want to try it on? It's probably too big, but we've got clamps."

"Sure."

In all honesty, she didn't want to be in the same room as a wedding dress, let alone wear one. The last time she had, she'd been trying on gowns for her own supposed special day, back in Springfield. The special day that had never arrived, the nonrefundable dress she'd never ordered, thank goodness.

But it's not a wedding gown. It's just a spangly, fun dress, and it won't be white, and why on earth can't you just let loose and have fun and be the center of attention for once? Because her heart hurt. Hurt as if somebody had cut it out and sewn a fistful of nails in its place. And she didn't feel at all like celebrating her singlehood.

Still, a lot of women would kill for this chance. And not too long ago, Lindsey would've counted herself among them.

"Are there shoes?" she asked, faking the excitement she wished she were feeling.

"Seven and a half, right?" James rifled through boxes and withdrew a pair of heels—silver and strappy with a stiletto that could murder a man.

"Whoa. I probably don't get to keep those, huh?"

James smiled. "Sorry. On loan from the designer."

"Oh, well. I'll always have the pictures."

Jenna arrived with an artsy man in tow, both of them carrying coffees. Her face lit up at the activity. She introduced herself to James, and Lindsey to the photographer, Ari.

Maybe if Lindsey could sell this idea that she was stoked to be single to the camera, to every person who walked past the newsstand… Maybe when she saw this cover… Maybe then she'd start to believe it herself. While the men strategized about the photo shoot, Lindsey showed the heels to Jenna, mustering a grin.

"Oh, *wow*." Jenna snatched one, nearly salivating.

"I know. Sadly, no chance I get to steal them. They're 'on loan from the designer,'" she added in a snotty, self-aggrandizing whisper. "So don't drool on it."

Jenna handed the shoe back. "Even if you did steal them, I'd steal them from you for my wedding."

"Speaking of weddings, check out what I'm wearing." James had draped the dress over a chair, and she held it up for Jenna.

"Hot damn."

"Not something I'd ever have picked, but yeah. Hip fairy godmother indeed." She clutched the bodice to her chest and let the skirt swish and flare. "Better make sure it fits."

She closed herself in the bathroom and stripped to her panties. With a deep breath, she unzipped the dress and stepped into it.

It was too big in the bodice, but she reached behind and clutched the extra fabric, watching herself in the mirror.

"Wow." The lights glinted off the clear and pearlescent sequins, and the wide satin ribbon around the waist shone like silver. Lindsey never wore strapless dresses, but now she wondered why—the cut made her shoulders and neck look terrific. *She* looked terrific. She looked...she looked like someone worth sticking on the cover of a magazine.

She looked like a bride.

A bride who'd misplaced her fiancé first, and now her lover. *Just a bachelorette playing dress-up in another woman's good fortune.*

She shook her head, alarmed the thought had even crossed her mind. As if there was anything pathetic about being single.

Then why a job as a wedding planner? Or a matchmaker, for that matter?

She'd never actually thought about it, how all her jobs seemed designed to celebrate the opposite of what this article said about her. She was supposed to feel empowered and liberated—that was the magazine's angle. But in all honesty, her singleness didn't feel like those things. Empowered and liberated were the things Rich had made her feel in bed, and with him gone, his body and voice and heat now thousands of miles away—

A knock at the door, then Jenna's voice. "Need any help?"

"No, just preening."

She took a deep breath and opened the door, holding the bodice to her chest.

Jenna's eyes widened.

"Does it look okay?"

"You look amazing."

"It's a bit big." Right on cue, James swept over with clamps, cinching the excess fabric at her back.

"Oh, yes," Jenna said, all breathy and overwrought. "That is… Wow."

James led Lindsey to the lights and reflectors angled around Jenna's desk. A stack of books had been arranged, their blank spines to be edited in Photoshop with titles such as "Etiquette" and "Chemistry." Lindsey would be perched next to said stack, with her legs crossed and one of the gorgeous shoes dangling from her toes, smirking and looking "mischievous and beguiling," as James explained.

Two women took over for Lindsey's makeup and hair. She admired the results in a mirror held for her, relieved they'd gone natural save for the fine, crystalline glitter swept over her lids. Her hair was done in loose curls, then arranged in an ethereal updo with a few dozen discreet bobby pins.

"Okay," Ari said, peering through his viewfinder and adjusting his tripod. "Sit on the edge of the desk for me so I can get a sense of the light."

Lindsey perched, and Ari blinded her with a flurry of test shots.

"Ready when you are," he said to James.

James hurried over with a paper box in hand. "The pièce de

résistance." He lifted out a tiara, glimmering like diamonds in the bright beams. He paused to fuss with Lindsey's hair.

"Oh, that's too funny!" Jenna said. "Hang on." She hurried to her bag and fished out a magazine, handing it to Lindsey.

The image socked her in the gut.

It was Rich. Starkly lit, stripped to his snug fighting shorts and championship belt, powerful arms locked across his chest. Chin tilted up, he issued the viewer an aggressive, cocky challenge, eyes all but lost in shadow. A crown sat at a careless angle on his head, a deep purple cape draped haphazardly over his shoulders, its ermine trim bringing out the white of the bandage at his temple.

The Prince Is King, read the bold cover copy. Love Him or Hate Him, Rich Estrada Is Light Heavyweight Royalty.

"Isn't that hilarious?" Jenna asked. "What are the chances you'd both wind up on magazines, wearing crowns? I'll have to frame them side by side."

Lindsey managed a laugh, but it felt as though someone were strangling her heart. All it took was a glance at that face and she was ready to fall to pieces. Worst of all, she was back to what she'd been for ten months—his fan, admiring from afar, from her impersonal spot among the masses.

Get lost in the shoot. This is your *time in the light. Don't miss it, dulling your shine for someone else.*

Someone she missed, deep down to her marrow, but someone who hadn't felt the same, not enough to change his plans. Someone with plans too *big* to change—certainly not for a woman he'd shared a few pleasurable nights with, a couple heart-to-hearts. Someone who shone so brightly, his memory left phantom auras burned across her heart.

They'll fade, she promised herself. *In time, they'll fade.*

James and Ari began issuing directions, and Lindsey scrambled to take them. She sat straight and got the shoe dangling. "Like this?"

James fiddled with her hair and bodice and posture, made her smile a hundred different ways—"Don't squint. Keep that chin down."

Perhaps mercifully, not long into the shoot he decided the tiara was "too literal," so it sat instead atop the prop books. The camera flashed and flashed and flashed, and Lindsey smiled easily through the opening shots. But she could feel her lips turning wooden. In the white chasing each flash, that image of Rich filled the void. With every frame, her hold on her emotions was slipping, a sharp and heated panic rising in her middle.

After fifteen minutes and a million adjustments and poses and blinding flashes, Ari called for a break so he could go through the first round of photos on his tablet.

Lindsey stood, uneasy on her feet, a ricketiness that had nothing to do with the heels. A head rush made her sway.

"You okay?" Jenna asked.

"I, um…" Her throat ached with brewing tears. "Sorry. This dress is so hot, and the lights."

Jenna hurried off to find Lindsey some water. Not eager to sit on the front steps and suffer the questioning looks of passersby, she thanked Jenna for the bottled water and excused herself to the building's rear exit for some air.

The wide alley was empty and she took a seat on the hood of Mercer's car, hugging the voluminous skirt in her lap. The morning was muggy, and in truth it was hotter out here than in the air-conditioned office, even in the shade. But it wasn't the heat that had her gasping for a deep breath.

She hurt in a way she hadn't felt before, a different pain entirely than when her engagement had been called off, or during any of her and Brett's breakups. It hurt like grief, every heartbeat echoing with loss. A tear escaped, chased by a half dozen more. She let them flow—venting this pain was the only way she'd get through the rest of the shoot.

This was supposed to be her day. Her chance to be the one at the center of it all. She'd expected to feel luminous and magnetic, and though that was how Ari and James and Jenna were treating her...it didn't hold a candle to how she'd *felt* with Rich's eyes on her, any of the times they'd enjoyed one another's bodies, even when they'd simply sat across from each other in that bar. In the end, she didn't crave an audience of ten or fifty or thousands. It had taken a single man to make her feel those things, and who knew how long it might take to meet another who could do the same.

She finished her water and forced deep breaths, knowing her break was running long. Right on cue, the back door squeaked, surely Jenna or James coming to coax her back inside. She stared down at her borrowed shoes, collecting her wits and praying the crying hadn't undone all the makeup artist's work.

Then she heard it—that familiar scuff and the clack of a crutch. "Linds?"

She looked up, as shocked as she might've been had an actual fairy godmother materialized to hover above the stoop.

"Rich?"

He hopped from the step and swung himself across the asphalt. "Jenna said you were out here." His gaze took in her getup. "She didn't say you'd be dressed like that."

"It's my shoot for the magazine." She blinked at him, confused. "You're back."

"I'm back. Whatcha doing out here?"

"I got overheated. Why are *you* here? Is your foot okay? Did your match get called off?"

"Foot's fine. Match is still on. Change of plans, training-wise."

"Oh?"

"You know that bit during the announcements, where they say, 'Fighting out of San Diego, Rich Estrada'?"

She nodded.

"Never sat right. So I'm back to fighting out of Boston. Out of Wilinski's." He nodded at the building.

Her stomach flipped. "You'd give up all those elite trainers and everything?"

He shrugged. "This place is my style. And my home. And if I can train down there with our misfit crew, and actually beat Farreira in November…it's good for everybody in that basement. It's good for my mom and my sister. And it's good for me, despite what my manager seems to think."

"Well. Lucky us. Um, welcome back."

He smiled and hopped closer, swiveling to join her on the hood. "But I'm not being a hundred percent honest."

"About?"

"About what brought me back," he said, eyes on the building. "I mean, it never felt right, fighting out of some flashy West Coast gym, but that didn't stop me from doing it the past year. Because there were exactly two people I could admit caring about. And in my head, caring about them equaled bringing home paychecks. But even with the money coming in…it hasn't fixed how I feel sometimes. Inside."

"Oh."

"I've got all these people who care about me—Merce and those guys. I didn't even want to see any of them when I got home. I didn't trust I was still worth anything injured. I kept everybody at arm's length. I kept *you* there. Like all we ever were was a good time."

She frowned. "Weren't we? To you?"

He looked to the fabric fisted in her lap. "No."

Her heart beat hard and her gaze, too, retreated into the ruffles.

"I wanted us to be," he said. "It'd make everything simple. But there's something about you. Something like a key that fits some lock in me, and gets all these thoughts spilling out, stuff I'd never tell other people in a million years. Those things I told you on the fire escape, and in bed, after…you know. I never talk to people like that."

His hand slipped between them, thumb rubbing at the hood's silver paint. "I've known Mercer more than half my life. He drove me to the E.R. in this car when I got concussed after a boxing match when I was seventeen. He let my mom have a nervous breakdown all over him in the waiting room. We lost a mentor together, and he came to my dad's funeral when I told him not to…. He gives so much of himself, I owe him what I would a brother."

"Sure."

He met her eyes, only for a second. "But I've never told him half the stuff I told you. Even if I *wanted* to be that open with him…it'd be like peeling off my skin. I couldn't physically do it."

"Oh."

"But I meet you, and this dark stuff just comes out. I get near you and the wall falls away. It scares me."

"Why?"

He sighed deeply, avoiding her gaze. "I'm so frigging terrified I'm not good enough to be what my family needs me to be. If I let someone else get close…I don't know."

Lindsey waited as he found the words.

"I'm scared of letting my mom and Diana down, but with them, there's no choice. Anyone else I might care about, I thought I could choose them, when the time came. When I'd done what I had to, when I had room for somebody extra. But I don't have any choice with you, either."

"I'm not sure I understand."

"I don't, either. I just know when I'm with you, when I even *think* about you…I feel like some different man. All broken down and defenseless, all this stuff I hate feeling, usually. This stuff that makes me worry, like maybe I might wind up with depression if I'm not careful. Like the kind that killed my father."

She squeezed his hand.

"Except with you, it actually feels good. Like all that emotional crap inside of me wants to get out, that stuff I can keep barricaded in with anybody else. And with you…I can rush around and try to plug all the holes you open up and try to keep it from escaping, or I can just let it go. Let it all out. And feel lighter, not empty, I guess." He met her eyes, looking confused. "Sorry. I'm no good with explaining feelings and shit."

"I think you're doing just fine."

"All the dark stuff, it got so much worse the second I landed in San Diego. I knew I wasn't where I was supposed to be. In my head, I was following the plan…but the plan doesn't work anymore. So here I am, I guess I'm saying."

"Because of me?"

He nodded.

As his words sank in, she felt as light and shiny as the dress, so light she might just float up off the hood and into the summer sky. "Wow."

"When I got settled back at the training camp, it took me two days to realize things were different. I always feel lonely at night when I'm away. Lonely, bored, restless. But this time I felt straight-up *sick*. Physically."

She rubbed his hand.

"I told myself it was Boston or Lynn I was missing. The familiar stuff, all the brick and the way it smells here in August. And that it was my family, after I got to see them for a couple weeks. That it was leaving the gym, believing I was actually giving back down there for the first time."

"But?"

"But it was you, more than all those other things."

She wanted ask, *Really?* But tears had her throat too sore

to get the word out. Rich coaxed her fingers from the tulle and took her hands.

He blew out a long breath and sat straight. "You wanna be my girlfriend?"

She laughed from pure surprise.

"That a yes or a no?"

She let a tear slip free. "That's a yes. I'd like that very much." Glancing down at the dress, she realized that for a wedding planner and matchmaker, this was all very mixed up. A question as delightful as a proposal but with nothing approaching its gravity, issued with her dressed for a jaunt down the aisle.

"Don't cry. You'll mess up your makeup." He dabbed at her lower lashes with his thumb.

"The past few days have been a roller coaster." But this changed so much of it.

He traced her cheek, fingers cradling her jaw. His kiss was as exciting as it had been last year in the back of that cab. It lit her up as hot and bright as ever, leaving her hungry when his lips finally let hers go.

For a long minute they simply sat, studying one another's face, fingers playing.

My boyfriend, she mused. *You're my boyfriend.* She smiled to herself, realizing how many women were going to hate her guts and feeling rather evil and pleased about it.

Rich asked, "How's your sister been?"

She sighed to admit that wasn't going at all to plan.

"I have a proposition for her, too."

"Oh?"

"If I offered to cover her dues and coach her personally, do you think she'd be willing to come back to train?"

Lindsey blinked. "Of course she would. Until September, like you promised?"

"I meant next summer, actually. For six months or a year, however long she needs to figure out if it's really her thing."

"You actually think she could make a job of it?"

He smiled. "I don't have the first clue. But I know it's something she wants to explore. Might teach her a few things about herself before she writes off college for good."

"I think she'd love that."

"Good. I'm prepared to commit to training her, on two conditions."

"Which are?"

"When she comes back, she's got to be able to run five miles without hyperventilating. I'm good, but I'm not a magician."

Lindsey laughed. "Fair. And the other?"

"She has to graduate."

Realization dawned. "Ah." She blinked at him, then grinned. "Aren't you clever?"

He shrugged, looking humble. "Just don't tell her I care. Last thing I need is for that girl to think I've gone soft."

"Deal." They shook, the gesture growing soft and playful, two sets of fingers flexing and twining.

He grinned down at the bundle of gauze and sequins in her lap.

"What?"

"That dress makes me wish I could carry you over a threshold."

She blushed. "It's a bit soon for that. I may not be eligible anymore, but I'm happy to stay a bachelorette for a while yet."

"How about you be my date to Jenna and Mercer's wedding, then?"

"That's at least a year away."

"I'm used to planning for events months in advance. Speaking of which, you better request extra time off to come to Rio Thanksgiving weekend. I want you right there in the front row, screaming my name when I step in with Farreira."

She bit her lip, imagining that moment. Imagining Rich winning, thanking her alongside the two other women he cared for the most. Striding next to him backstage, warmed by that spotlight, not lost in its shadow.

Speaking of lights. "I better get back inside before the magazine goes broke paying for the photographer to sit around twiddling his thumbs."

Rich stood and helped her down, and she unlocked and held the door for him as he hopped up the step.

As they made their way down the hall, he said, "I want to forbid you from even finishing this shoot—letting every man in Boston believe he's got a chance with you."

She raised a brow. "Do you, then?"

"But I'm pretty sure that kind of caveman shit would get me punched."

She laughed. "It might."

"So instead maybe I could just watch?"

"I don't see why not." She wondered how different the two sets of photos would look, the before shots when her heart was still broken, the after ones with her face lit up, her eyes finding Rich's between flashes.

Those dark eyes, across a room. Across the country, coming through a TV screen, or gazing from halfway down a fire escape, or burning up at her in bed. This extraordinary man, somehow hers. Somehow asking to be a part of *her* audience.

She put her palm to his back as they turned the corner into the foyer. Warm muscle beneath her fingers, warm summer sun glittering through the dress. Warm nights ahead even as the weather grew cold, with a man who lit her up, from the inside out.

* * * * *

Have Your Say

You've just finished your book.
So what did you think?

We'd love to hear your thoughts on our
'Have your say' online panel
www.millsandboon.co.uk/haveyoursay

- 🌹 Easy to use
- 🌹 Short questionnaire
- 🌹 Chance to win Mills & Boon® goodies